HOWL PLAY

THE SPELLWOOD WITCHES, BOOK 2

MELANIE SNOW

Spirit Paw Press, LLC

CONTENTS

The Spellwood Witches Series

Witch's Tail

Howl Play

Tail of a Feather

Impawsible Mischief

Pawtrayal

Howl Play

The Spellwood Witches, Book 2

ISBN: 978-1-7324375-7-9

ASIN: B08H5WKTWB

(Spirit Paw Press, LLC, Concord, NH 03303)

www.wendyvandepoll.com/melanie-snow

Thank You

Download Your Free Gift

A Welcome to Witchland Map

Thank you for purchasing *Howl Play, The Spellwood Witches, Book 2*. To show my appreciation and because of a popular request from my readers,
I am offering a:

Welcome to Witchland Map

Just in case you forgot to download in Book 1, please download here.

https://wendyvandepoll.com/melaniesnowgift

SARAH OPENED HER EYES. THE FIRST RAY OF SUN pushed through the bedroom curtains, adding a tinge of warmth to the cold gray of the tiny upstairs room. In her fuzzy pajamas, underneath the thick quilt and flannel comforter, she could only feel the morning chill on her nose and cheeks.

Sarah smiled as she realized she thought of this little room and bed as hers. It had been several months since her entanglement with the nasty real estate developers and Dismas Lorian. Already she had fallen into a rhythm, a routine of comfort and harmony. She had even started to sleep upstairs in Michael's old bed again, having solved her former mentor's murder and apprehended Dismas the Hunter, a hired environmental surveyor with his own personal vendetta to eliminate endangered lynx from the woods, who had killed Michael when he had gotten in the way. Solving the murder had helped her vanquish her fear of the stairs on which Michael had died. Every corner and curve of Michael's house was becoming familiar to her, as if she had always lived here. Her life as an overworked New York City attorney squished into a tiny office and an even tinier apartment, scurrying for taxis or fighting crowds in the subway—it now all felt like a dream, like something that had never truly happened to her.

Addie stretched alongside Sarah; her ears flopped across the quilt adorably. Even in sleep, it was now obvious that she was no ordinary dog; there was something far too human, too sharp, in the expression on her sleeping face. She bolted upright, a split second before the sound of a knock.

"Margaret's here," Addie remarked.

Sarah cracked a grin. Already she was able to understand Addie without the Leekins—those pesky little faeries who finally became allies when they helped Sarah save Witchland. Sarah loved the long conversations and running narratives of her little life shared with Addie in Michael's cottage. Sarah was also starting to be able to talk to plants on her own. As a novice witch, she found delight in balancing her magical studies with her legal career and her new forays into environmental law. Though law and magic seemed to be polar opposites, Sarah was melding them together to achieve her passion, preserving the Witchland Forest.

"Rise and shine!" Margaret hollered shrilly.

One thing Sarah had not yet grown accustomed to was how her neighbors—and, indeed, most people in Witchland—rose at the very crack of dawn. They had so much energy without even a sip of coffee!

"Hi," she said wanly, pushing the door open.

"You ready?" Margaret chirped, all energy and smiles.

"I thought we might do it a bit later in the day." Sarah shifted, feeling the comfy bed upstairs calling to her still.

"No! This is the best time for potion-making! When the plants are happiest, the most eager to give." She took Sarah's hand and started to pull her to their cottage next door.

"Hang on! I need to get dressed!" Sarah protested.

Margaret glanced down at Sarah's fuzzy fleece pajamas with their little clouds and sheep. "Oh. Right. Well, hurry! We have a lot of work to do!"

Sarah pulled on some clothes in a hurry. Then she met Margaret out front and followed her to the neighboring cottage. Addie trotted along behind them.

"This is going to be fun, Sarah. And don't worry, I'm here to give you moral support," yipped Addie.

Sarah always felt enveloped in warmth and love whenever she entered Margaret and Hua's humble cottage. There were plants everywhere—beans sprouting on the table, herbs growing on windowsills, exotic vines covered with an abundance of fragrant, jewel-like flowers snaking across the backs of chairs and up the walls, a greenhouse behind the main house that was so densely packed with plants of all varieties that it was almost hard to breathe inside its jungle-like fragrance and humidity. Their house and greenhouse felt like perpetual summer, while their garden had embraced autumn, with colorful squashes and pumpkins swelling at the end of verdant vines. The sense of abundant life and joy suffused the entire property, adding the vibrations of so many little plant spirits to mingle with their own.

"Good morning!" Hua breezed into the kitchen, her colorful kimono swirling around her slim frame and her face full of energy and pep. "Hi, cute puppy!" She beamed and pecked Sarah on the cheek and gave Addie a kiss on her nose. "Are you sure you're ready?"

"Well, I'm still half asleep," Sarah admitted sheepishly. "But I've been dying for our first lesson. I've been putting it off because, well, I've been incredibly busy with studying." The memory of long nights buried in environmental law books and paranormal books gave her a headache just thinking back on them.

Hua waved her excuse away, but Margaret peered at her, clearly unconvinced. Sarah did not like how Margaret searched her face, seeming to read things that lay under the surface of her smile. Both women were eerily perceptive, but Margaret tended to give Sarah chills with her intuition.

"Do you have any injuries?" Hua asked first.

"Um?" Sarah began searching her body. Finally, with Addie's help, she located a tiny bruise on her ankle. She was in awe of her dog, who could sniff out anything with her nose. In fact, it was Addie's nose that helped her locate Dismas, the Hunter, in the dark woods at night and, thus, solve the lynx case and Michael's murder.

"Perfect! Now watch that bruise and take a sip of this." Hua thrust a tureen toward Sarah. "It is best to instruct the plants in the potion to do what you want, by the way," she added.

The potion tasted like warm carrot ginger soup. As its tingle spread down her throat to her stomach, Sarah instructed the plants to help heal her. Before her very eyes, Sarah watched the purple of the bruise fade and finally vanish into the milk white of her inner ankle. A tiny freckle on her ankle now stood out, chestnut once again. She gasped. "Wow! This stuff really works!"

"It is one of the simplest recipes and incantations you can learn—but it works. It is still magic, herbal magic. This is our first lesson today." Hua began to teach Sarah the various components of the potion and how to speak to the plants and prepare them.

As Sarah gathered her supplies, she repeated the spell Hua just taught her because she didn't want to forget a thing:

Cauldron is light
Cauldron is bright!
Bring these plants of healing
Forth to their rite!

As Sarah stirred the bubbling soft orange potion in the little cauldron, she asked, "Are there any plants that are magical? You know, like mandrakes and such?"

Margaret and Hua exchanged looks. "Mandrakes are extremely rare and hard to come by these days. We have been trying to obtain one for many years," Margaret finally said. "I found one. When I was hiking in Wales. He screamed bloody murder when I asked if I could harvest him. Of course I did not go any further. You cannot harvest plants without their consent. They give you their lives as a gift; only then can their essences provide any healing power."

Sarah smiled, sadly but fondly remembering the plant who had attempted to sacrifice its life for her in the doctor's office when it had launched itself at

Dismas's head. Without it, she might not be standing here today. Thankfully, the plant had been repotted, but its willingness to die for her made her heart swell with gratitude.

"If you take plants against their will, you put their pain and suffering into your body, and it defeats the purpose," Hua went on. She pointed at the bubbling cauldron. "When you make your own potions, you unlock some of the healing power, too. You put your heart and soul into everything you make, everything you cook and bake. Half of the magic of herbalism is within; it is not just up to the plants."

"But I can feel the plants! I can feel their presences," Sarah said. "I always have, since I was a little girl."

"Of course you can." Hua smiled. "Some people can't, but you are a Spellwood and the direct descendant of Lativia Spellwood, the greatest witch of all time! You are a very powerful empath, and that is where much of your power comes from. You can feel and sense things hidden from most people."

"Maybe that's why I was so unhappy in New York," Sarah mused. "Too many people, too little nature."

"And now you are here, where you always belonged," Margaret said happily.

"I'm glad to be here. Even if there are challenges ahead. I feel this was meant to be," Sarah affirmed.

When Sarah finished her potion, Hua cut herself slightly with a piece of paper, hissed in pain, and then sipped the potion. The cut vanished before their very eyes.

Sarah stared incredulously. While she had looked forward to this lesson, she also had not quite believed that she could do it. She didn't imagine that her little ordinary self could pull off the same powerful magic, the "impossible" things, that Hua and Margaret could do with herbs. Yet here was the proof that she had abilities. An incredible sense of pride overtook her, even greater and sweeter than her very first victory in court in her third year of law school.

Suddenly, a thirst for doing more rose inside Sarah. "This is incredible!" She gasped. "What about telekinesis? Or casting off hexes? I want to do more!" She realized she sounded like a child at Christmas and felt embarrassed, but she could not curb her enthusiasm anymore.

Hua gently shook her head and cautioned her not to try too much too soon. "You don't know how to manage your energy and protect yourself. You will easily get far too fatigued."

"I really want to try more," Sarah urged.

The women exchanged glances. "I suppose I can

teach you a spell to help you camouflage yourself in the trees," Hua offered helpfully. "It's an old Spellwood trick, actually, and fairly easy. It won't wipe you out."

The two women led Sarah into the woods and coached her. Sarah was thrilled to go outside and learn to disguise herself within the trees.

"Now, when you look at the trees and ground around you, you must bring the image into your mind. Feel it. Become it," Margaret explained. "Then chant this spell." She handed Sarah a slip of paper with a spell scrawled on it. "This imagining and the spell together help you take on the images of the surroundings. When you do that you can blend in. You can't be seen then, and you can't be heard, because your very essence is part of the surroundings."

Sarah glanced at her. "Um, that sounds awfully simple."

"It is," both women said frankly.

"It sounds unimaginably hard to me!" Sarah exclaimed.

"Try it," Hua urged. "It's really not that bad."

When she had a clear image of the trees' energy in her mind, Sarah tried to imagine herself looking the same. She began to read the spell scrawled on the paper aloud. Then she glanced at the witches, wondering if it had worked. Nothing felt changed to her.

"It's okay. Try again," Margaret urged.

Sarah tried ten times before she sighed. "Ladies, I give up. I think you need to teach me some other way to do this."

"You are overthinking it," Margaret said kindly. "Please take a deep breath and meditate on the trees. Clear your mind."

Sarah did as she was instructed. Slowly, she breathed in, relishing the scent of the forest, desiring to become one with it. She was able to bring that energy into her body as she inhaled deeply. As a result, she faded into the trees, appearing as a part of them.

"I did it!" she cried joyously, her disguise vanishing as her concentration broke. "That's amazing!"

Margaret and Hua cheered. "Now practice that every day," Hua told her, "and you will be able to do it effortlessly, like we do." To illustrate her point, she and Margaret both camouflaged themselves so that Sarah could not see them at all. "You can also blanket this spell on others to protect them," Hua added, her seemingly disembodied voice sounding eerie. The two witches began to appear again, grinning at each other in pride at their skill.

As they returned to the cottage, Sarah couldn't help but feel that there was more powerful magic the witches were withholding.

Margaret could sense her disappointment with the

generic magic lessons of the day. "Don't worry. Soon you'll be impressing us, Sarah Spellwood."

Sarah smiled, stuffing her impatience down inside of herself. "Patience is a virtue, I suppose."

"We're herbal witches, so we can only teach you about plants and such," Hua added. "If you want a well-rounded education, you should really do your own research and seek out mentors in other kinds of magic."

"How? Where can I possibly start? You are the only witches I really know!" An image of Harriet in the pointy hat and her snarky crow flickered into Sarah's mind. "Except for Harriet; I won't go to Harriet for this!" She felt utterly overwhelmed at the thought of teaching herself anything in this elusive field, a field she had not even believed in just a short while ago.

"It won't be easy," Margaret began cautiously.

"A lot of trial and error," Hua agreed.

The two women exchanged looks.

Then Hua snapped her fingers. "You know? I think Daisy has Lativia's original spellbook! It's the real thing that Lativia wrote, not just copies like most of us are learning from. You should try her apothecary. Ask her to show you a thing or two. She's an herbal witch as well, but she knows a lot about other types of magic."

Margaret began to tell Sarah where the apothecary was, but Sarah smiled and interrupted, "I know exactly where that place is." She had felt a strange pull to the old shop and the eccentric lady who ran it, but had never found time or reason to venture inside until now. She had kept meaning to, but the past few months since arriving in Witchland had not exactly been calm and lazy. She had her fair share of cases to work on, and now she was studying environmental law *and* learning to be a witch. It was harder than law school!

One thing she did know was that Daisy would remember her. Warm memories of watching Daisy stir things in a cauldron while her dreadlocks danced with each whisk and spin of the mysterious liquid—and, of course, laughing at ribald jokes with Aunt Beth— swirled in her mind. Daisy had once given her a leather-bound journal and told her to always write her innermost thoughts in a cipher. That way no one could ever steal them from her. "Your ancestor, Lativia, did the same," Daisy had said.

After that, Sarah studied the cipher of Beatrix Potter and used that in her journal. She loved writing in code and decorating the margins of the pages with doodles of animals and plants and hearts, particularly when she was bored in math class. The cipher was especially helpful when she developed her first crush on a boy in her third-grade class, who she wrote about profusely. One of her classmates taunted her, "Sarah and Bobby, sitting in a tree!" then stole her journal and attempted to read it to the whole class, only to be frustrated by the clandestine symbols inside.

"I think it's time we visit Daisy once again and see what other helpful life tips she has for me," Sarah told Addie. "Besides, I wonder if she still smells like powdered flowers. I always loved that scent as a girl." Returning to Daisy's would almost be like returning to her aunt Beth's. She had been incredibly heartbroken when Aunt Beth passed away twelve years ago.

Addie wagged her tail excitedly. She clearly knew who Daisy was, too.

CHAPTER TWO

Sarah intended to go to the apothecary, but she worried she might cry, being so close to the memories of Aunt Beth. Her aunt's passing had left a gaping void in her soul and Sarah had a hard time dealing with the grief. As hard as she tried nothing had ever completely filled the void. Though she looked forward to seeing Daisy again, she decided she needed to confront her grief first.

She decided to blow off some steam by taking a run through her new town with Addie first.

"Ya know, Addie, I really can't believe that I left my boring real estate attorney persona and became a protector-of-the-forest witch, as well as an environmental lawyer. It's completely out of my comfort zone," Sarah mused as she ran. Though it was a temperate fall morning, sweat was already beading on her neck, under her untamed mass of red curls. As her feet hit the cobblestones of the town square with deliberation, her muscles began to stretch and awaken, and her lungs strained, making her feel alive.

"Isn't this a much better calling than real estate law, though?" Addie mused as she loped smoothly alongside Sarah.

Sarah loved how practical Addie was, always putting life in perspective. "It is better . . . more purposeful. It's a serious step *out* of my comfort zone, so much so that I have no clue what I'm doing! Without Michael as my mentor, I'm definitely having to figure all of this out for myself." Mentioning Michael made her feel sad again; the grief she experienced over his murder still haunted her, day and night, though she felt better now that she had put his killer away for good. Dismas Lorian, the Hunter, had just received sixty-five years for the first-degree murder that he had admitted to on recording for Sarah, as well as for his attempted murder of Sarah, poaching the endangered lynx species, and tampering with evidence.

"After what you managed to do for this town already, I think you have more than enough grit for the job," Addie said warmly. She was always comforting Sarah in this way, her true nature as a loyal and loving familiar shining through her canniness.

"It is overwhelming at times, but it sure isn't as bad

as some of the nasty court cases I have fought and won," Sarah agreed.

As they quietly ran together, Sarah took in the town. It was remarkably quaint, complete, and neat. From the cleanly swept streets to the cottages and shops that all linked together, sharing walls but maintaining their own artful and charming fronts, the town had a spirit unlike any Sarah had seen before. It was quiet, yet a sense of liveliness seemed to pop beneath the surface of the entire village. Now Sarah knew what it was: Magic lay underneath the town's very fabric. Trees had begun to color richly, and autumn wildflowers bloomed in planters between them, a testament to the Leekins and the townsfolk who both loved and tended to nature.

Winded from her jog through the crisp air, she finally reached Lativia's Javacadabra. The scent of hot espresso and freshly baked muffins oozing buttery sweetness lured her inside, her mouth watering.

Zeva, the white feline who was a sort of poster cat for the coffee shop, walked across the countertop to her favorite spot next to the cash register. She neatly wrapped her tail around her sleek body and pushed her whiskers up to reveal her pointed fangs, her version of a friendly smile. *"Hi, Sarah,"* she said sweetly, punctuating her salutation with a purr.

Addie wagged her tail, ready to tease the cat. But

Zeva barely glanced at her, ignoring her as usual. Sarah scratched her under her chin and cooed, "Hi, Zeva. How's it going, kitty kitty?"

"Pretty well. Karen swatted me out of the croissants this morning. The butter in them smelled so utterly delicious, I thought it was quite unkind of her to not offer me some," Zeva complained, as she commenced licking her paw.

Susie shook her head and told the cat, "You can't be in our bakery items! We go over this every time!"

"You could at least offer me a taste." Zeva sulked.

"You know I always do, but Karen does things a little differently. She just doesn't want to get in trouble with the health inspector, and you know that." Susie sighed. Then she beamed and turned to Sarah, chirping, "A green tea latte, my dear?"

Sarah liked having someone who remembered her drink order. That never happened in New York, where the crush of people around her made her anonymous, even to the barista she saw every single day at the bistro near her old apartment. "Sure thing. Thanks, Susie!" she said.

"How's my favorite doggie?" Susie asked Addie, who replied that she was having the best day of her life, as she always did.

Susie was the only other person Sarah knew— besides her late Aunt Beth—who spoke freely to animals; Margaret and Hua could speak to plants, but they did not speak to animals as easily without using spells to open communication. Susie had been able to speak to Zeva, whom she had adopted from a shelter in Vermont, without even drinking a magical potion. She was the one who had explained to Sarah one day that Addie had been Michael's familiar, an animal tasked with helping him with his magic and witchcraft. Now that he had passed on, Addie had moved on to assist Sarah with the same. Zeva was Susie's familiar, making her the only expert on the subject that Sarah knew.

As Sarah waited for Susie to finish steaming the milk for her tea latte, Susie excitedly told her about how Claire was going to visit. "You remember that story I told you, about the magical little girl who stole all of our cookies one Christmas to give her mom a nice Christmas and Zeva caught her? Well, that's Claire. She's in college now, and she's coming to visit during her break before fall term." She grinned. "Magic and mischief will abound!"

"That's great! I want to meet her." Sarah smiled warmly. She personally related to the story of Claire, the spooky little girl with green eyes who could make snow stop falling and who could magically abscond with Christmas cookies from a locked bakery to give her single mother a nice holiday; Sarah herself had once been like that as a child. "I hope college doesn't make her lose touch with her gift. That's what I did—I repressed my gift to become a lawyer."

"That's partly why we keep in touch, though I also consider her, her mother, and her stepfather a part of our family," Susie explained. "I want her to keep up with her magical education. So far, she has retained her gift and even used it to memorize her textbooks while sleeping."

"I wish I had known how to do that; it would have saved me from the long library hours in law school," Sarah grumbled jokingly.

The door in the back of the coffee shop, which led into a small library of used books for the taking, jangled open. Sarah glanced up and froze when she recognized Daisy. Daisy had recently dyed her dreadlocks purple and wore them in a massive ponytail high on her head, making her look even more regal and magical than usual. She was wearing a robe that swirled around her, seemingly of its own energy.

Daisy strode toward her. "Sarah Spellwood," she said, a huge grin spreading across her face as she peered at Sarah through her purple-rimmed glasses. "How I've wanted to see you!"

"How did you know it was me?" Sarah laughed breathlessly. Then she realized what a stupid question that was; everyone in this town knew everyone!

Daisy stooped to scratch Addie behind the ears.

"You look just like you did as a little girl. And, of course, you also greatly resemble the portrait of Lativia in the town hall," she admitted. "I kept up with you over the years from afar. Michael sure talked about you a lot."

Sarah felt honored at this mention of her former mentor and how he had bragged about her to the whole town long before her arrival. "I was actually intending to come talk to you today. Hua and Margaret told me to seek you out."

Daisy stood back up and grinned. "Then, get your drink and come on over. I'm just opening up." She turned to Susie, who already had Daisy's customary chai tea ready as well as Sarah's tea latte.

The two women crossed the courtyard into the apothecary. The apothecary was adorable, made of all natural wood and full of plants hanging from the ceiling. Its air was rich with a spicy scent that Sarah could not place. Three of the walls of the shop were completely lined with shelves bearing jars, all full of strange dried or powdered plants and mushrooms Sarah couldn't name. All manner of liquids, oils, and powders filled the large glass case at the head of the apothecary.

"How have you been?" Sarah asked, taking in Daisy's appearance as she unlocked the front door. It was good to see her, like seeing an old friend.

Daisy beamed. "I have been doing amazingly well. Doing what I love every day. And you, Sarah, you've grown to be a beautiful woman!" She cupped Sarah's face in her hands for a moment and looked her over. "You are just gorgeous now."

Sarah flushed. "Thank you."

"I see you've found your way back to your natural affinity for magic. Finding yourself after being lost is such a glorious feeling, isn't it?" Daisy smiled as she began to ready the shop for another busy day.

"It is," Sarah agreed, thinking back fondly on how her life had changed since coming here. "But also, a bit confusing. I have a lot to learn. Which, of course, is why I'm here."

"Tell me, what would you like to know?" Daisy asked.

"Anything you can think of to tell me," Sarah requested, shrugging helplessly. "Margaret and Hua taught me a camouflage spell and how to make a healing potion."

"Those are important. But I imagine you want to know more about the logistics of it, don't you?" Daisy jolted Sarah back to summer afternoons at Aunt Beth's, when the two of them would shock Sarah with their acute intuition.

"I think that would be helpful to start," Sarah agreed.

"Most witches belong to a coven. Covens are just stronger; it's like teamwork makes the dream work, but in magic, of course," Daisy explained as she bustled about, setting out herbs and pestles. She permitted Addie to join her behind the counter. Sarah marveled at how everyone in Witchland welcomed animals. "Your relative, Lativia, was in the Wolf Coven. So was her sister, Madras. Originally, anyway."

"You have to tell me more," Sarah said eagerly. She had never heard of Madras or even considered that Lativia might have siblings.

Daisy hesitated. "Lativia will tell you more when it's time," she said cryptically. "Sadly, Madras was burned in the Salem Witch Trials, but Lativia settled here and watches over the town to this day. It can still be possible to speak to Lativia, in spirit."

Sarah knew better than to press about Madras. "Can I have a short magic lesson, at least something very brief?" she requested softly. "Please?" she added, reminding herself of a tiny five-year-old wheedling to get more candy. That's how delving into magic felt to her, like getting pieces of candy.

"Let's go over some fundamentals, shall we? But that's all I can do today. I have several formulas to make for customers, and the natural Viagra can be quite time-consuming," Daisy answered.

Sarah laughed. "I guess people can't go without

their natural Viagra!" Then she added, "Thank you so much, Daisy." The experience reminded her of her first time in court, when she had breathlessly sought to prove herself to everyone and learn how to be the best lawyer she could be. Doing her best and learning made her heart soar, filling her with a fervor for life.

Daisy began to explain as she set out jars and boxes on the counter for the day's work, "Magic is not something some people are gifted with and others aren't, like in *Harry Potter*. There are no muggles. We're all capable of magic. But some people have such guards up against it, such an inability to tap into their gifts and their intuition, that they might as well be muggles. You are fortunate to have family members who are very strong magically, meaning that you are better able to tap into your skills."

"It's hereditary?" Sarah had often wondered if she could even possibly be like Lativia, when she felt so ordinary, like just another human walking the earth, bound by the laws of space and time.

"Somewhat. As I said, we all have the ability. But only some of us are willing, and able, to tap into our abilities. We have to be . . . sensitive. Imaginative. See, magic transcends all reason, logic, and physics. It defies the rules we are taught to believe about our world, because those rules are not really true. All of the rules you have been taught to believe limit you, restrict you, keep you from using your powers because you think it is impossible. From the time you were a baby, you were conditioned not to believe in magic, which made it harder and harder for you to tap into your skills as you grew older."

"That makes a lot of sense. How did I tap into them? It all started on Mount Katribus. . . ." Sarah still got chills as she thought of the first time she heard Addie speak and saw the ground erupt with Leekins from beneath little pine cones. Mythical beings she had never even known about had made her doubt her sanity for a while. Now she knew what a special day that had been, a gift really.

Sarah looked at Addie with fondness, who perked her ears at her, and said, "*Sarah, introducing you to Clover Figcreek and her Leekins was one of the best days of my life.*"

Daisy said, "Something about the Leekins and Mount Katribus was able to infiltrate your mind and spirit and make you more sensitive to your intuition. After you took the Leekins' potion, you started to awaken your natural magic. And trust me, you are not alone in uncovering your powers up there! I know this because many other people come to me and report what happens to them after taking that potion; Michael was one of them. Astounding things happen up there all the time." Daisy began to crush herbs in a press for some pills she was making. "Those Leekins are some remarkable beings, I'll tell you that. The real event was that you were able to break one of the rules keeping your powers caged—the rule that you can't talk to dogs, or trees, or all of the other animals and plants and fungi in our world. But you can talk to anything if you match the right vibration. It becomes a sort of link between your spirits."

"Like telepathy," Sarah suggested.

"Exactly. Except it's not so much magic as being sensitive, in tune, in harmony. Being on that mountain helped you become synchronized with nature, and you were able to connect to an entire world you never knew existed before." Daisy smiled up at her. "It is a truly special experience, isn't it?"

"It was stunning," Sarah agreed eagerly.

Daisy kept smiling as she returned to her work. "You know, you really must ask Hua to teach you about interacting with trees using your natural Spellwood powers. You see, that's another thing. All of us can be magical, but, like some people are better at math or English, or some people are better at painting or writing, witches and warlocks have special strengths. Interests. Skill sets. Most of us feel drawn to one form of magic and then stick with that."

"Like Hua and Margaret, herbal witches," Sarah said, beginning to understand more and more.

"Yes, exactly, and me, too. Now, as a Spellwood"—she grinned and shook her head—"boy, you can really be the savant of magic! Lativia certainly was. She even created her own spells that many of us, myself and Margaret and Hua included, still practice to this day. As her descendant, you are especially able to develop strengths in several forms of magic, making you a very powerful witch indeed."

"Me?" Sarah did not believe that she was particularly skillful or powerful in anything magical. But when people hinted that she was, thanks to her lineage, she always felt awed and impressed by whatever lurked under the surface of her abilities.

"Yes, you." Then Daisy sighed. "I can tell by how you carry yourself that you have no confidence in your abilities yet. You have no ability to gauge the depth of your power. You don't believe in yourself, and that makes you feel quite weak. It is normal for a novice witch to feel this way; the feeling of powerlessness fades with time and practice. I urge you to keep learning and practicing, and one day, when you really need your powers, you might just shock yourself with how powerful you really are."

Sarah took a deep breath. "Is there some . . . exercise? Something I can do to help get some confidence? I want to learn everything perfectly!"

"Try this." Daisy set a bottle on the counter. "You see it is empty, right? Nothing in it."

Sarah nodded.

"Now picture that bottle in your mind. Close your eyes tight and get a mental picture. Do you see the bottle behind your eyelids?"

Sarah nodded again as she concentrated on the blue bottle in her mind's eye.

"Now imagine it full of whatever you like and say:

Bottle of blue

Fill up your queue

With (anything you wish to fill the bottle with) through and through!"

Sarah briefly opened her eyes. "Like a liquid?"

"Anything at all!" Daisy was watching Sarah intently.

Sarah shut her eyes again and imagined the bottle filling with some dried chamomile flowers in a bag resting on the counter. She imagined a few tiny flowers would spill over from the mouth of the overfilled bottle.

"Imagine harder. You have to really believe that the bottle is full," Daisy urged.

Sarah peeked and was disappointed to see the bottle was still empty. She snapped her eyes shut tight again, focused harder on the image, and said the incantation with more force.

Bottle of blue
Fill up your queue
With chamomile buds through and through!

She told herself it was real and reached out to touch the mouth of the bottle. When she felt chamomile buds under her finger, she started, and her eyes flew open.

The bottle was completely full of the flowers.

"How—what?" she stammered.

Daisy grinned. "You have that Spellwood ability to manipulate time and space with your mind's eye. But it is still very hard for you. One day, you will be able to do it without thinking so hard about it or even closing your eyes."

"Amazing," Sarah murmured.

Addie wagged her tail and barked. *"And you thought you weren't made for this duty as protector of the forest,"* she quipped.

Sarah beamed, pleased with herself. She had never felt so good in her life, not even when she had graduated from law school.

As she went to leave, Sarah remembered what Hua had told her. "Oh, one last thing. Can I see Lativia's spellbook, please?" she asked, turning with her hand upon the lavish gold doorknob.

Daisy sighed heavily. "Sure, you're welcome to it, but it's blank."

Sarah cocked her head quizzically.

"See for yourself," Daisy said as she directed Sarah outside and through the courtyard, into the small room of curiosities and books behind the coffee shop. There was a locked glass bookcase containing wands of all shapes and books, bearing a sign in capital letters advising people to handle the items with care. Daisy unlocked it and located a heavy leather-bound book that looked rather inconspicuous compared to the others. It released a puff of dust and smelled slightly of mold as she opened it. She began to turn the pages, and, sure enough, there was nothing but blank paper, yellowed with age.

"You see, this is the table of contents." Daisy pointed to the first several pages of tight, spidery writing with neat page numbers. "But the rest? Nada." She brushed through hundreds of pages to stress her frustration.

Sarah ran her finger over the paper, trying to feel for depressions from a pen. But the pages were smooth, as if they had never borne words. "This is unusually strange," she muttered under her breath.

"Obviously, this is magic," Daisy explained. "Some

sort of disguising or blocking spell. But for the life of me, I can't figure out how to undo it. I've tried all of the traditional counterspells. I've even tried researching very olde magick—the spells of the Middle Ages and before—that we don't really use anymore. Nothing."

"Hmmm, thank you." Sarah nodded in disappointment. "I'll see if I can find out more. Maybe I can unlock the writing, as her relative. May I borrow it for a while until I can figure it out?"

Daisy made a gesture that seemed to say, 'Be my guest.' She added, "I love creativity. Magic is an art form, not a science. You can do what you like with magic—with some practice, of course. I like to add bits of hoodoo and voodoo from my lineage in Haiti, for example. If you can experiment and find a way to unlock this book, then I think you earn the right to keep the book, especially as Lativia's descendant."

"Thank you," Sarah said warmly. "And if I can't unlock it, well, how do you learn Lativia's spells?"

"Most of them were passed down orally, and some of us in the Wolf Coven have written them down over the years. These transcribed spells obviously are not as pure as the original—because things get lost in oral tradition, of course—but they still work. I can teach them to you, as can Margaret and Hua," she replied warmly.

Sarah's phone then buzzed with a text. Her heart

jumped into her throat when she saw Officer Eli Strongheart's name on the screen. "Gotta run Daisy! Have a great day!" she called as she hurried out of the shop, Addie at her heels and the heavy spellbook tucked under her arm.

"What could he be saying? Do you think he's finally asking me out?" she asked Addie.

Addie just looked at her, as if to say, 'You're ridiculous, and stop smiling like that every time you think about or see Eli.'

But when Sarah opened the text, hoping for some form of flirtation, her high mood rapidly dissipated.

"There's been a suspicious death. The town clerk," the text read. "Please hurry," said a second one she received as she already began to jog in the direction of the town hall.

"*No dinner?*" Addie asked.

"Nope." Sarah felt both apprehensive and terrified.

"*Something bad happened,*" Addie said intuitively —darkly. "*Someone is dead, huh?*"

CHAPTER THREE

Sᴀʀᴀʜ sᴛᴏᴘᴘᴇᴅ ᴀᴛ ʜᴇʀ ʜᴏᴜsᴇ ᴛᴏ ᴘᴜᴛ ᴛʜᴇ ʜᴇᴀᴠʏ spellbook on her desk for later, then she pelted toward the town clerk's office, her chest smarting with the effort in the cool air. The sun warmed her skin pleasantly, but she was no longer paying attention to the lovely scenery of the town. She was too anxious about whatever evil awaited her at the town hall.

The front of the grand old building was cordoned off with yellow crime scene tape curled around its carved marble pillars, looking glaring and unnatural. The mayor stood out front, speaking with Eli, while the New Hampshire State Police Major Crime Unit, the attorney general, and the coroner milled in and out of the open oak doors of the town hall.

"Sarah! You made it!" Eli said when he spotted her. He gestured for her to join him and the mayor.

"You have unfaltering intuition, so I knew you could be an asset here today," he said. Then he began to scratch behind Addie's ears, her favorite spot. She began to twitch in joy.

"He is cute," Addie teased Sarah, her eyes shut and her mouth open, tongue hanging out in pleasure from his scratches.

"He sure is," Sarah responded silently. *"But I have a job to do, and I'm not going to let him distract me!"*

Sarah felt flattered as she blushed violently.

"Sarahhhhhh! Stay focused," reminded Addie.

She tried to steady herself, keenly aware of how Eli was staring at her with a little smile on his lips. She glanced around, desperate to get serious. "Looks pretty pristine. What happened?"

Just as Eli began to explain what had occurred, Mayor Lewis interrupted to greet Sarah. She had not seen him since her first meeting with him, John Gonforth, and B & M Real Estate. *Has he always looked this awful?* Sarah wondered. He was gaunt, gray, and shaken as he related how he came into work, unlocked the office, and found the town safe open with no sign of the clerk. He then went outside and discovered the clerk lying in the alley by the trash cans, apparently mauled by an animal. He became incoherent at this point, breaking down into tears. Hastily, he wiped away the tears as well as the beads of pallid sweat that had collected on his forehead and were staining his collar.

"Do you want to see this?" Eli asked Sarah.

Sarah thought back to the only other dead body she had ever seen, which was Michael's body in crime scene photographs Eli had shown her. While it was disturbing, she knew she could stomach this. Also, she wanted to impress Eli with how tough she was. She nodded.

Eli led Sarah around the hall to the body. There was even more crime scene tape and people standing around taking pictures. Though the body was covered respectfully in a sheet, Sarah could sense pain and death emanating from it. There were a few bloodstains marring the gray concrete around the body, and Sarah noticed the glint of the clerk's watch on his wrist, poking out from under the sheet.

"*I sense the same feeling as when Michael died,*" Addie said forlornly.

Sarah put a comforting hand on her head. "*It doesn't look like an accident, does it?*"

"*Not at all,*" Addie agreed. "*I knew someone died again.*"

Sarah felt bad. This must be very traumatic for Addie, remembering Michael's death. "Can I go inside?" Sarah asked Eli.

"Sure." Eli led her and Addie into the office, the

mayor trailing anxiously behind and wringing his sweaty and shaking hands.

Sarah looked around the neat little office. Investigators were taking pictures of the safe hanging open. Some keys lay on the desk, with a numbered evidence card next to them.

"Was the safe robbed?" Sarah inquired.

"It was, actually. The safe held ten thousand dollars, as well as the original deed to the town," Eli answered.

"Who would want to steal the deed?" Sarah was puzzled. "Wouldn't that be pretty worthless?"

"Here's the thing. That deed was . . . um, it was stating Lativia Spellwood held the title to Witchland," Eli explained, scratching his head.

Sarah was taken aback. "Lativia holds the title to Witchland?"

"She did," Eli explained.

"News to me as well," Mayor Lewis muttered, a bit bitterly. "I'm the mayor. Shouldn't I know these things?"

"The title isn't what we're worried about." Eli shook his head. "The problem is the death. And the fact his keys were on his desk, yet someone had locked the door behind him—or her. That means that whoever robbed the safe already had keys to the town hall."

Sarah felt the hairs raise on the back of her neck. "I

don't understand why the death even happened?" she mused. "If someone had keys, why kill . . . um?"

"His name was Mr. Atticos," Eli and Mayor Lewis said at the same time about the town clerk. "Greek for bad luck," the mayor added, pointing out the bitter irony.

"He lived next door, in a little apartment above that antique shop. He worked late and seldom was home. His family had always lived here, but he was an old widower, and his children live out of town. He often spent time alone here, looking after the town, looking into history. In fact, he was a bit of a local history buff," Eli said, indicating the piles of dusty old tomes on the man's desk. "There was nothing he didn't know about this town, or the Salem Witch Trials, or really all of New England. Anyway, it was not unusual for him to be here all night long by himself."

"This is odd," Sarah remarked, approaching the safe. Everything in the office seemed peaceful, undisturbed, except for the small bit of dust missing from the top of the safe.

"There are no fingerprints, Eli," the police chief's deputy, Jenna, spoke up. She startled Sarah, who had not seen Jenna approach from behind. "They used gloves, whoever it was."

"No fingerprints on the keys or the safe?" Sarah asked.

Jenna shook her head, then turned to Eli. "Why is she here? We can't have her contaminating the crime scene."

"I thought we could use her help. She was sure instrumental in the Michael Howler investigation." Eli shot Sarah a charming smile.

Jenna looked crestfallen for a moment. Then she turned to Mayor Lewis. "Mayor Lewis, with all due respect, would you mind accompanying me down to the police station?"

"I already gave my statement," he replied defensively.

"Yes, but you failed to mention that you were the last person to sign out of the building last night," Jenna said. "Mr. Atticos never signed out, which means you two were here working together—quite late, I might add."

"I can explain! I was working on some old property deeds—" The mayor faltered when he realized the suspicion with which Jenna was regarding him. "I'll come down to the station," he said, resignation and apprehension mixed on his face. "I'm just not feeling good."

"Dead bodies can make you queasy," Eli informed him. Then he instructed Jenna, "Get him some food and cold water at the station. And a towel." Eli glanced at the sweat stains blooming under Mayor Lewis's armpits.

"Ten-four, Eli. And thanks for your help," Jenna told Sarah, a bit curtly, as she followed Mayor Lewis out of the office, a firm hand on his back.

Eli touched Sarah's elbow, sending tingles up her spine. "You okay? You look a little sad."

"I don't think Jenna wants me here," Sarah said forlornly. She had never been great at connecting with other people on a personal level, and so she usually did not have many friends. At some deep level, however, she yearned to befriend Jenna and have more girl friends in general. But her intuition noticed the way Jenna looked at Eli, and the sharp glances she often tossed the two of them, and she had a feeling why Jenna was so standoffish with her.

Eli immediately confirmed her theory. "Jenna . . . she can be territorial. Especially of me. Since my divorce, she has been particularly protective of me, like a big sister."

Sarah raised her eyebrows. "You don't think she likes you?"

"Jenna? Oh, no, of course not." Eli seemed caught off guard. "We're partners, after all. Why do you ask?" Eli seemed ready to change the subject.

"Just a gut feeling I get." Sarah shrugged, eager to also change the subject.

Eli looked uncomfortable. "Look, I'm single as can be." He held his hands up, and Sarah realized there was a reason he was telling her that, which made her stomach twist and turn into happy knots.

But Eli was a serious man, especially on the job. He seamlessly moved on to going over his theory of what had happened in a different tone. "Jenna is right to question Mayor Lewis, but he didn't do it."

"How do you know?" Sarah was surprised at the conviction in his voice.

"Because there was animal hair on the body and bite wounds. He was mauled, apparently by a wolf, though the crime lab has to verify that."

Sarah frowned. "A wolf? That's impossible."

"How so?" Eli seemed genuinely interested in what she had to say, something she was not used to from her first marriage, when Jeff would dismiss her as a silly woman.

"I've been studying wolves, and they are quite misunderstood. But they very rarely attack people, and never in this scenario." She was becoming increasingly suspicious that a wolf was being framed and was not the actual culprit.

"Interesting." Eli nodded, processing her words. "Not even if he felt threatened? Or had rabies?"

"I need to look into rabies more, but no, not even if he felt threatened. They are more scared of us than we are of them. And with all of the woods and abundant prey around, there is no reason they would come into town like this," Sarah reasoned.

"Hmmm, that just makes this all stranger. Maybe someone had a dog or wolf trained to kill? That's possible," Eli mused. "All I know is there was no reason for Mr. Atticos to be outside. We're not sure of the time of death until the medical examiner determines it, but his body was pretty stiff with rigor mortis. We think he had been out there for several hours, probably since last night. We think maybe he was in the office and something lured him outside. The perpetrator broke into his office, used his keys to access the safe, then locked the door behind him, giving away one heck of a good clue that he's on the inside. Somehow, in the interim, a dog or wolf of some kind killed Mr. Atticos. Unfortunately, it really doesn't look too good for Mayor Lewis at this time. I don't think he killed the clerk, but he sure looks guilty for stealing the money."

"I just don't think any of it adds up," Sarah continued, shaking her head. "And I am sensing some bad vibes just looking at the scene. I sense . . . something ominous."

In a desperate murmur, Eli explained, "I agree. Anything to do with Lativia usually has to do with magic, and I worry the deed was maybe magical. I think you need to go see Clover Figcreek and the other

Leekins. I have a hunch that that deed isn't just a deed, and now you say the clerk didn't just get mauled by wild animals. It's time to put your new knowledge to work, Real Estate-Turned-Environmental-Paranormal Lawyer Spellwood and your sidekick, Addie the Super-Smart Dog."

Sarah giggled, loving her new title. The way Eli said it warmed Sarah's heart.

"*I'm more than just a sidekick,*" Addie grumbled privately.

"*It's still a compliment,*" Sarah replied to her telepathically.

"I'm all for this investigation," said Sarah, realizing that she was now involved in another murder investigation. Though solving mysteries was stressful, she was thrilled to be considered useful and to bring justice to Mr. Atticos. Everything about the case was shifting very quickly, and Sarah felt that she needed to step back in order to make sense of it all. But she could also sense that there was far more to this than a simple murder and robbery.

"No, but you might be the rightful heiress of the entire town," Eli went on. "Your life could even be in danger now."

"People don't own towns," Sarah argued, trying to ignore the valid point he had just clearly made.

"Lativia *did.* And I'm not taking any more chances

on your safety—on . . . ah . . . the *town's* safety." Eli cleared his throat. "Please, Sarah, I have a crime scene to close. The town hall needs to open again and be back in business. We can tackle this crime while the evidence is still fresh. Can you go speak with Clover Figcreek again? At least for my peace of mind? If it's just a deed and there's nothing magical going on, then we have nothing to worry about."

Jenna returned to the office and looked slightly irritated to see Sarah still standing there. "Thanks for your help, Sarah, but I really need to get this scene processed." She eyed Addie. "I can't have dog hair contaminating my crime scene, sorry, Addie." She affectionately patted Addie's head, and Addie wagged her tail. She understood, with her typical good nature.

Eli gave Sarah a look and guided her out of the office. When he placed his hand on the small of Sarah's back, she felt the pounding of her heart. She loved the warm pressure of his hand, ever so slight, barely there yet so noticeable that it was all she could think about.

"I better let you get back to work," she said slowly, reluctant to leave this moment. She loved how the sun made his eyes pronounced, like the water in a cold creek.

He smiled, then turned serious again. "Please go visit Clover Figcreek."

"I will," she promised. "Right now."

"Can we meet later?" he went on. "Javacadabra?"

She looked hopeful. "Sure."

"To go over what Clover Figcreek said," he added hurriedly, smiling awkwardly.

"Sure, sure." Sarah couldn't help but feel a little disappointed. She wanted him to ask her to dinner so badly, so she could get lost in his eyes over candlelight. But the idea of seeing him later added some pep to her step.

Addie glanced at her judgmentally as they headed in the direction of the mountain. *"He is cute and wonderful, and I like him, too, but you can't let him distract you. You just saw a gruesome crime scene, and you are acting like it's the best day of your life."*

"Sorry, I just can't focus on a ghastly crime scene when I'm near that man," Sarah defended herself, though she could hear how silly she sounded. "You know I haven't had anybody love me since . . . well, since my ex-husband just walked out. He didn't even tell me why or what was wrong. I felt unlovable for a long time after that—paranoid that I would ruin any relationship I touched, and now this guy . . . well, he makes me feel like maybe I can be desirable and likeable."

"Of course you are desirable and likable! But being too distracted can deter from your intuition," Addie

cautioned. *"You could miss some clues, or something important Clover Figcreek has to say. Focus."*

Sarah knew Addie was right and tried hard to clear her mind as they approached the rotten old fence where the Leekins hid in the pine cones and Michael lay in peace in his grave. But when she thought of Eli's smile, she became distracted all over again, a fuzzy feeling taking over her body. How badly she wanted to get to know him better!

She tried to clear her mind and prepare for her meeting with Clover Figcreek, the leader of the Leekins. The Leekins were faerylike beings who protected the forest, its creatures, and the whole town of Witchland. After her work with them on stopping Dismas from eliminating the endangered lynx from the forest, they had vowed to always help her in any endeavor that had to do with Witchland's sanctity. They would surely know what to do in this scenario.

Sarah reached the old fence and called out softly, "Oh, Leekins! Clover Figcreek!"

Slowly, they began to emerge from the underbrush, the holes in the fenceposts, and the pine cones littering the ground. Swarms of them massed near the fence or buzzed through the air on little brown wings. They began to form a pyramid, and Clover Figcreek ascended on top.

"Yes?" she demanded, her hands on her hips.

"You know how you said you would help me if I ever needed it?" Sarah began.

"This had better be important," Clover Figcreek replied. Then she added begrudgingly, "Yes, what is it?"

"Well . . . Mr. Atticos, the town clerk, was attacked —and it looks like murder. And the town deed is now missing from the safe," Sarah explained.

"You really are sure? The deed is nowhere to be found?" Clover Figcreek demanded.

"Yes, it's nowhere to be found," Sarah replied grimly.

Clover Figcreek's chocolate brown skin started to turn deep blue as she yelled out, "Eeeeeeeowwww!" All of the Leekins underneath her began to tremble and sob as they also turned blue.

Sarah winced, hating the annoying shrillness of the Leekins when they panicked and grieved. Though she had come to admire and rely on the creatures, she still did not necessarily like them. She was grateful that they had ceased to infiltrate her house and mess in her business, as they had happily done before she had won their trust when she had first gotten to Witchland. They had even rearranged all of her furniture and Michael's files after she had finally set up Michael's house the way she wanted it!

"Oh, no. No, that's not good at all." Clover

Figcreek began to fuss. The other Leekins also began to rub their hands together fretfully.

Addie cringed, also hating the sight and sound of the Leekins in distress. Their squeals hurt her ears.

"What does it mean?" Sarah was getting very worried, too.

"Lativia cast a protection spell over the town. But because the town is too fluid—people moving in and moving out, buildings going up and coming down, trees dying and new ones growing—she couldn't put a permanent blanket spell over everyone and everything that would endure the centuries. So she had to lock her spell inside of an object, and she chose to use the deed. With it gone, there is nothing defending Witchland from evil magic, nothing at all," Clover Figcreek explained, her voice high with anxiety.

"Who would want to use evil magic on the town?" Sarah was puzzled, but she also kept thinking of the weird, ominous feeling she had gotten from the alleyway behind the town hall.

"You will have to speak with Lativia today. She will explain it all and what you must do," Clover Figcreek said decisively.

"Lativia has been dead for centuries," Sarah said awkwardly. *Hadn't Daisy also mentioned something about talking to Lativia? Surely they can't all be serious? Am I supposed to talk to the dead now, too?*

Clover Figcreek blinked. "So?"

Addie interjected here, "*Leekins can speak to the dead all they wish, whenever they want. Mortals, however, either have to possess strong medium abilities or else they have to go to a place where the veil between our worlds is thinner—easier to pass through.*"

"And that place is . . . ?" Sarah didn't like the sound of talking to a long-dead relative. As fascinated as she was by Lativia, she also believed the dead deserved to rest in peace, and communication with them was far too magical for even her comfort at this point in her witch training. What would she say, anyway? Lativia was surely intimidating! The most notorious and revered witch in New England, possibly even the United States, was not someone to cough at!

"*The top of Mount Katribus! Remember what Daisy told you about meeting Lativia?*" Addie said, clearly exhilarated at the prospect of a long walk up the mountainside. Like any dog, she loved long walks and chasing the scent trails of squirrels. Sarah did not yet realize that Addie also wanted the chance to maybe see Michael, her former person.

The Leekins and Addie started to lead Sarah up the mountain. It was now late afternoon, approaching sunset—not the best time for a hike, but, regardless, the air felt delightfully crisp, and Sarah began to feel more at ease. Addie bounded around ahead of the group, sniffing rocks eagerly, chasing rabbits and squirrels, bouncing eagerly from tree to tree. She never strayed too far, though, and Sarah knew she didn't have to keep a leash on her.

"Michael and I used to explore all of these woods with the Leekins," Addie reminisced excitedly. *"When he began to really get into using his powers, he would climb to the top to commune with the ghosts and speak to Lativia. They became good friends."*

Something about Michael speaking with her long-dead relative made Sarah happy. Michael was practically family to her, anyway, sometimes more of a dad than her own dad, who was a criminal defense attorney and often too busy to answer her calls home. "You must really miss him," Sarah said. She often forgot to consider how heartbroken Addie must be; she lost her person, her dearest companion.

"He is always with me," Addie replied, and chills ran up Sarah's spine.

"How can that be true? I thought we mortals could only speak with them at the top of the mountain?" Sarah asked, confused.

"Some of the dead can choose to leave the clearing where the veil is thin, if they have a strong attachment to someone." Addie continued walking along blissfully, tongue rolling out and tail wagging. She did not realize how much she had just shook Sarah, who now yearned

for Michael to come down from the mountaintop and be with her always, as well.

"He was attached to me," Sarah said, a bit stung. Then she realized how petty she sounded and changed her tone. "I guess I just need to learn how all of this works. Just a few months ago, I refused to even believe in ghosts!"

"He watches over you, too," Addie reassured her gently. *"Those weird vibes you felt in his house were his spirit trying to tell you to look into his death more. And the peace and happiness you felt after solving the case was partly Michael, at peace himself. You just can't see him yet because you need to unlock your abilities to communicate with the deceased."*

Sarah felt a flicker of hope warm her chest. "Will this trip to the top of the mountain help me with that?"

"It will if you let it," Addie said, wagging her tail and lolling her tongue cheerfully. Like a typical dog and a quintessential familiar, she was happy-go-lucky even when talking about something somber. Death did not bother her as much as it did humans because she knew it was not the end of someone's spiritual life.

"Did you not see ghosts as a child?" Clover Figcreek asked Sarah.

Sarah reflected back on her childhood in upstate New York, where she lived with her parents in an old stone house. As far back as she could remember, she would see the old man in some kind of war uniform, though which war was unclear to her young mind. He would grin at her at night as she was falling asleep, and sometimes he would sing her lullabies. Sarah called him "Grandpa" because her own grandfathers were both deceased by the time she was born, and he filled the role for her. She never feared him. She would tell her parents about how kind he was, to which they would hastily and nervously inform her, "Honey, ghosts aren't real."

Her father was the direct descendent of Lativia and had grown to resent the Spellwood name and the notoriety that came with it. He had never used any magic, or so he claimed, and he made fun of his sister, Beth, for her strong witchcraft practice. Sarah's mother was always reassuring Sarah that her powers were fantasy, likely because she was trying to convince herself of the same fact. Only at Aunt Beth's visits did her parents let loose a little, helping Aunt Beth make potions in her giant cauldron and talking to ghosts on the Ouija board. Back home, everything would become serious again, and after Aunt Beth passed on, it was always serious.

"If you want to be taken seriously in the world, you can't go around acting like a typical Spellwood," her father explained to her in middle school, when she came home crying because everyone was chanting

"Abacadabra!" at her in the lunchroom. "You have to stick to the facts, the things people can see. Witches are still persecuted these days, maybe not burned at the stake, but persecuted nonetheless. I learned that first-hand in college when I couldn't get a job because of my reputation as a Spellwood. Your mother taught me to be rational, and life has become much better." He had added the last part with a strained smile, as if he were lying.

Sarah snapped back to the present. "Yes." She smiled slowly. "I did see ghosts as a kid."

"Then you already have the medium ability, but you have buried it, like most adult humans do. Magic is like any skill—if you don't use it, you lose it. You just have to open yourself up to the ability and practice and you will be able to see ghosts all of the time," Clover Figcreek explained.

Sarah shuddered. "I don't know about seeing them all of the time. . . ."

"Only the ones who have a strong attachment to you or really need to speak with you will show themselves to you. Trust us, ghosts prefer to sleep if they can," another Leekin, named Shamus, piped up.

An idea suddenly made Sarah grin with hope. "Is my aunt Beth up there? I would love to see her again!"

Clover Figcreek looked annoyed. "This is not the

time for chatting with your whole family tree! We have pressing issues to deal with!"

Sarah did not say anything back, but she nursed a steady glow of excitement to see both her former law mentor and friend, and her beloved aunt.

CHAPTER FOUR

Eventually, they reached the top of the mountain, where the trees grew denser. There was very little light at all, but wildflowers and moss blanketed the ground, green plant life somehow resistant to the perpetual chill of the peak. Though the plant life was green, it also seemed to glow with a strange blue luminescence that filled the air. Sarah's hair stood up on end all over her body with the eerie prickle of electricity. The sensation only became stronger as they trekked farther through the gloom.

Suddenly, they entered a glade, and there were dozens of ghosts! They looked like people, but they were completely transparent, surrounded by a blue glow that was quite ghostly. They were milling around, holding up goblets of blue wine and nibbling little blue cakes from a long table floating in the center of the clearing. All of them were smiling and laughing.

And in the center of the great crowd stood Michael Howler. He was unmistakable, even though he was now see-through and blue. Sarah drew in a sharp breath that hurt slightly. His face felt so good to see!

Addie yipped in joy and ran to him, cutting through the bodies of other ghosts, who turned in mild surprise to survey her. These ghosts were used to the living joining them for communion with long-dead relatives or friends; they were also used to dwelling among the forest creatures. The presence of an excited dog was not a particularly shocking event for them. When they looked past Addie and saw Sarah and the Leekins, they also did not seem very perturbed.

Sarah stopped, aghast, heart hammering. How she had missed her mentor's kind face! He looked exactly as he had the last time she had seen him, frozen in the same age for eternity. His graying hair hung down to his shoulders and looked tousled, his flannel shirt was unbuttoned at the collar and a bit wrinkled, and he even had on his half-moon glasses perched on the tip of his nose, like John Lennon. Just the way she remembered him. She was so overcome with joy and grief that she did not know what to do with herself.

"Go hug him!" Clover Figcreek urged her. "He

won't hurt either of you. Ghosts like to know that they are remembered and missed."

Sarah lunged toward Michael and threw her arms around him in a warm embrace. Her arms shot right through him, and she lost her balance, almost falling through his body. It felt like running through cold electricity; jolts shot through her nerves, chilling her to the bone, but not in an unpleasant way.

She realized she was crying as Michael smiled at her, taking the sight of her in. He kept one hand on Addie's head, somehow able to touch her when he could not touch Sarah. Sarah realized it must be because of Addie's powers as a familiar and her profound connection to Michael that kept him in solid form for her. It was clear how much he had missed them both in the other world, since his life had been taken from him prematurely.

"Here we are," Sarah finally gulped through her tears. "Finally. I've wanted to say hi to you one last time so badly."

"Oh, me, too," Michael said, shaking his head slowly. "I wondered how long it would take you to find me." He looked past her shoulder at Clover Figcreek, who was exchanging greetings with several ghosts she knew.

"I'm sorry it's been so long!" Sarah wiped the tears from her face, but more followed in a furious torrent.

This moment was so extraordinarily happy and painful at once that she could not entirely cope with her emotional turmoil.

"Has it been a long time?" Michael seemed genuinely surprised. "I am asking because I have no concept of time, really. Sometimes it is lighter than other times, but it is always dark up here."

"It's been over three months," Addie told him.

"Oh!" Michael's eyes widened. "I suppose that seems about right. I keep track of you two, you know. I like to check in now and then. But I don't keep track of the days. I've heard you talk to me now and then," he went on. "I always respond, but you never hear me." His face turned sad then.

"I hear you," Addie said loyally, wagging her tail and trying to get closer to him. Her hair was blowing up around her, as if frizzled by static electricity. *"I love you so much."*

"We both miss you—badly," Sarah sobbed. "All of Witchland misses you."

Michael looked heartbroken. "I miss you all, too. I wasn't ready to go. Not yet. I loved my life, my cottage —" He ceased talking, the grief choking him, as he gazed at Sarah and Addie with tears in his eyes.

"Do you like the memorial we all built?" Sarah asked, desperate to change the subject before her heartbreak overcame her.

"Oh, yes!" Michael bowed his head humbly. "It was a bit much, to be honest with you. You didn't have to put me by the old Wolf Coven house! It's too much of an honor. I really didn't do that much for the town compared to others."

"You really don't need to be modest," Sarah said. "You started something amazing that we have to finish. You took protecting this town to a new level, a legal level, and you helped me find my calling in life. Your death actually brought me to my destiny, I think. You deserve all the honor and recognition in the world for that."

"Thank you," Michael said, continuing to be modest but also clearly flattered. "I also must thank you for finding out what happened to me, and not just believing it was an accident."

Sarah sniffled. The pain of Michael's life, snipped short by a greedy, evil monster, still felt like a stab wound in her chest. "I couldn't just let you die without justice," she assured him. "It was no trouble at all. You would have done it for me."

Clover Figcreek flew up to Michael and touched his hand. Her tiny brown hands also did not pass through him. "It is so good to see you again, Michael. I brought Sarah here to speak with Lativia."

"Ah, yes, I figured as much." He smiled wryly.

"You're in for a real treat. She's one of our oldest and wisest."

"Surely there are older ghosts?" Sarah asked.

"There sure are, but most of them move on when they are no longer needed on earth. When their every cause has ended and their every relative has died, they have no more purpose here and finally enter eternal rest. But Lativia, well, she still has a job to do, as do I. We stay—keeping an eye on things, offering assistance when we can. Lativia is responsible for all of Witch-land, so she will be here for a long time, longer than most of us. It must be exhausting for her, really."

"Come on, let me introduce you," Clover Figcreek urged.

Sarah hated to stop chatting with Michael, but she felt the impending cold of night crushing into her. She was sadly unprepared, without even a heavy coat. She tenderly hugged Michael again, even though her arms went through him, and then followed Clover Figcreek to the back of the clearing.

There, next to the long feast table, was a throne woven of tree branches, bedecked with flowers, and cushioned with rich moss. A woman who looked just like Sarah sat upon it commandingly. Her curly red hair swirled around her face, cast in a blue sheen, and her piercing green eyes sparkled smartly. She wore a long white robe embroidered with hummingbirds and blossoming vines, clasped at the hollow of her throat with a gold and ruby brooch.

Lativia smiled at her gently. "It is nice to see you up close," she said in a surprisingly husky voice.

"You, too," Sarah said awkwardly. She felt awestruck to be in the presence of this notorious witch and uncertain of what to say. She added, "What do you mean, up close?"

"I have seen you through my crystal ball," Lativia responded.

Sarah felt mortified. *When have you been watching me with a crystal ball? Have you seen me do something embarrassing?*

Lativia seemed to read her thoughts and gave a gentle laugh. "Don't worry, I am not spying on you, only waiting for you to wake up to your calling, your true self. It's a shame that society—and your father—kept you away from magic for so long. Your father could have been a glorious Spellwood, but instead, he sits in his study and reads law books for fun."

Sarah laughed, picturing her father with his growing bald spot, sitting in his recliner and listening to classic rock records on an expensive turntable stereo while reading tomes that even she, also a lawyer, found mercilessly dull. Imagining him as a glorious warlock was impossible. Then again, he was probably a master at repression, just as she had been not too long ago.

"Toward the end, when Michael died and the Hunter came too close to killing all of the lynx in this forest, I became rather impatient for your arrival, I must admit. I needed you to take over Michael's work, and I knew that I needed your physical presence to save the forest; I am too old and growing too feeble to do much physically anymore." Lativia held up her ghostly arm. "I used to be able to shove people and knock things off of shelves when I needed to."

Sarah nodded. "I'm here now."

"It's just a pity that Michael had to die to bring you here, but destiny always works out in strange ways. And all lives serve a good purpose, if not many. There are good people and there are evil people, but we all have a bit of both within us. And if not for evil, then good would not be as beautiful or as precious."

"Speaking of evil . . ." Sarah began.

Lativia sighed. "Yes. I gravely understand my deed has been stolen and another precious life has been taken over greed."

"I recognize this theft is bad for the town. What can I do?" Sarah implored.

"First, you must learn to harness your true magic." Lativia leaned back in her chair, preparing for a long story.

"I've been learning the Spellwood trick, to blend in

with the trees. And I've been learning potions," Sarah said hopefully.

Lativia sighed again. "I am happy that you are learning what you can. That is the Spellwood way, to make do with what you have. But sadly, that trick of blending with trees is only the very beginning. There is so much more to our magic that Daisy and Margaret and Hua can't teach you because they don't know it themselves. They simply have not developed the skill or the power. Many of my teachings have been lost or diluted over the years."

"They mentioned we Spellwoods have a lot of power, power to do any kind of magic," Sarah said.

"That is true. But we also have strengths, areas where we excel best, like any witch. That is why witches do best in covens, where they can draw on the unique powers of all of the witches. See, Spellwoods aren't herbal witches," Lativia explained. "We have the ability, sure, but we deal more in . . . fauna, over flora. Our strengths are best used in that realm."

"You mean . . . spells relating to animals?" Sarah was confused.

Lativia waved her hand, a gesture that meant she would get to that. "As Daisy told you, I had a twin sister, Madras. She was burned at the stake, but I escaped, thanks to my shapeshifting abilities and the help of the Wolf Coven. They banded together to save us, but only were able to save me. My sister had gotten into evil magic; she was a good person at heart, but the temptation of power got to her, and she succumbed to . . . dark influences. The Wolf Coven could not save her unless she renounced her ways of gloom, but she refused. Hence, she is now a dark and evil ghost, who died long before me.

"I founded the Wolf Coven as a way to embolden women in a time when women were regarded as little more than house slaves. I wanted to preserve the witch magic that Puritans persecuted and let women take back the power they had been robbed of. We are the strong ones. We can do everything men can—and also what they can't, which is bring forth life from our bodies. We strike fear in them, so they convince us we are weak and silly and irrational and hysterical." She laughed disparagingly. "Men have strengths, too, but they often rob us of ours just to feel better about themselves, and that was why my coven was hated. That is why *witches* themselves are unfairly hated.

"Wolves had bonded to women of my coven in ancient times and had vowed to always protect them—and their descendants—throughout the centuries. We aligned ourselves with wolves and protected them, as well. It became a bond that has never faded. That's why Addie here is so good to you," she concluded.

"Because she's a dog? And dogs are close to

wolves?" Sarah looked to her beloved friend, who stood beside her. Michael lingered behind her, his hand still hovering over her back.

Lativia smiled. "Because she *is* a wolf."

Sarah turned to see Addie, the sweet golden mixed-breed, start to morph into something broader, bigger, with a more massive jaw and glowing silver fur. And behind her, Michael began to transform as well, with silver fur erupting from his skin and his nails turning to giant claws. He finished transforming into a much larger wolf than Addie, and the two stood looking at her, wagging their tails expectantly and proudly.

Lativia explained to a shocked Sarah, "Everyone has an animal spirit, and members of the Wolf Coven happen to have wolves as theirs. When Michael and Addie came here, they were made into official members of the coven. That is a high honor for a man to be trusted enough to be let into the coven, and Michael earned that honor. Now they can both transform into wolves if they must. It is a power bestowed upon them by our wolf friends."

Sarah gaped at them. "Can I turn into a wolf?" she asked slowly.

"If you will take up your torch as a protector of the wolf, and this forest, then yes. You will be fulfilling your ancestral duty, a duty I took on many generations ago. You will become a member of the coven and take my place eventually, too," Lativia informed her.

"But what am I supposed to do?" Sarah asked, feeling bewildered and, frankly, terrified. This seemed like such a lofty duty!

"You first must clear the name of the wolves who are being accused of this murder. You and I both know wolves don't attack humans. They are being used as a scapegoat. Sarah, find the true criminal behind it all," Lativia urged.

"But there haven't been wolves in this forest for ages." Sarah had become familiar with the flora and fauna of the area in her research into environmental law. Understanding the geography, history, and biology of the region was imperative to protecting it in court, lest she sound like an incompetent idiot.

"This forest holds more than it is willing to show. But you are a Spellwood witch with high intuition, which makes you more adept than the most skilled FBI agents at sniffing out the truth. You can talk to animals, as well, which makes you privy to secrets most people will never learn in their lifetimes. Turn to the many resources you have at your disposal to truly become a Spellwood witch." She indicated Michael and Addie, still in wolf form, with a sweep of her ghostly arm. "They are all here for you, those two and many others, volunteering their own special powers for you to make into something complete. Draw on the strength of the coven! Don't just learn about herbs; learn it all."

"I will try my best," Sarah said warily. She had the sense she was accepting a task she could not possibly complete, and the heaviness of being overwhelmed settled into her limbs, making her feel rather dizzy. Plus, she liked learning about herbs from Hua and Margaret; knowing that they could not help her as much as she had thought made her feel discouraged about her magical studies.

Then, an idea occurred to her. "Speaking of resources, couldn't your spellbook come in handy? I can't read it. No one can."

"It likes music. That's why all old spells rhyme, you know, because they're really songs to be sung to music," Lativia said flippantly.

Sarah narrowed her eyes. "But what kind of music? I'm supposed to just play music to it?"

"You have much more in common with the wolf spirit than you think," Lativia went on. "You are cunning, clever, determined, all of the things you need to be to save this town. I have full confidence in you, but you need to find your inner wild woman and believe in yourself. Now, I must go, for my time here is limited. It's taking more and more out of me to stay here conversing with the living as more time passes since I died. But you must come see me whenever you are in dire need and I shall lend you what help I am able."

"How dire? I feel like now is pretty dismal, and I have very little information. . . ." Sarah trailed off as Lativia's ghost faded, its bright, glowing form dissolving into the gloom. She then realized she was very cold indeed, and very alone, at least as far as learning about how to become a witch.

Michael was also fading as she turned to say goodbye to him. "Goodbye!" she called, a fresh sheen of tears filling her eyes. It almost felt like losing him all over again as he lifted his hand in farewell before entirely disappearing into the darkness.

"It's always sad when the party is over! But you still have friends in the village who won't fade away into the gloom!" a familiar voice said cheerily behind her.

Sarah spun around. There Aunt Beth stood, her flaming red hair drawn back in a bun at the nape of her neck and an apron covering her gingham dress, only a crystal necklace around her throat offering a clue that she was more than just some old lady who liked to bake cookies. She looked exactly like she did in Sarah's memories.

"I'm so glad to see you!" Sarah gushed, moving to embrace her aunt. Then she hesitated. It had been over twenty years since she had last seen Aunt Beth, ailing in her bed, and she did not know what to say.

But Aunt Beth's jovial face was already beginning to fade. "I can't stay long now, dear, but I want you to know that you are on the right path and I believe in you! All of those days talking to my goat certainly paid off, didn't they?" She chuckled lovingly as only her outline remained visible. "I love you, always."

Feeling disheartened that she could not spend more time with her lost loved ones, Sarah stood in place for a long time, staring at the spot where Aunt Beth had been. All of the other ghosts began to recede into darkness, their party with the living over for now as they returned to the other side where they dwelled.

The cold seeped into Sarah's bones, and she realized she was violently shivering. Gradually, she turned and left the empty clearing with Addie. Sarah eyed Addie, who was still in wolf form, instinctually feeling leery of her muscular haunches, piercing yellow eyes, and large fangs. Never in her life had she been this close to what appeared to be a wild animal. She felt relieved when Addie began to morph back into her more familiar dog form as soon as they left the heavy magic of the clearing, plunging back into the earthy, mossy scent of the forest.

"I didn't really want to ever leave," Sarah admitted sadly. "I wish I could bring Michael back with us."

"*I do, too,*" Addie said, her voice thick with grief.

"No one ever does want to leave," Clover Figcreek said. "But the living and the dead must be separated, or what would be special about living at all?"

"I guess none of us really know," Sarah mused, in a strange mood because of all of the revelations and experiences she had just had.

For the rest of the hike down, she, Addie, and the Leekins remained in silence, each dealing with their own parts of the puzzle of this crime. Sarah wondered why Lativia didn't answer her question about the music, and she nursed her regret that she had not hugged Aunt Beth. She felt like sobbing into her pillow at home instead of taking on a murder mystery and saving Witchland from evil, once again.

CHAPTER FIVE

By the time they reached the bottom of the peak, it was twilight and quite chilly. The challenging hike down had warmed her, but the tip of her nose smarted and her fingertips stung. She shoved them deep in her pocket and bid adieu to the Leekins, who urged her to seek their help whenever she needed it.

"Can you tell me what else you are hiding from me, girl?" she asked Addie. While she was attempting to be good-natured toward her loyal canine companion, she also felt like her head was spinning with all of the information she had to now process, as well as the huge lack of information she felt this meeting with Lativia had left her with. As a result, her tone came across slightly sharp.

Addie looked at her reproachfully. *"Don't get*

snarky. I had to wait until you were ready to see my power animal spirit."

"How do you guys all seem to figure out when I'm ready for things? Do you have secret when-to-tell-Sarah-things meetings every morning?" Sarah continued to sound slightly irritable as she fished out her phone and texted Eli to meet her at Javacadabra.

Sarah's heart plummeted when she noticed Eli was not waiting for her alone at the coffee shop; Jenna sat across from him, already enjoying a cup of steaming cocoa.

Eli smiled at Sarah, then glanced around to ensure the coffee shop was empty. He then asked her how it went with Clover Figcreek and the Leekins.

Sarah shot Jenna a look. "She knows?" she asked.

Jenna shrugged. "I've been here a lot longer than you have." Then she softened, realizing how sharp her tone was. "I know there is a lot that goes on around here that can't be explained by your run-of-the-mill science. I would be a bad cop if I didn't entertain the possibility of magic in a place called Witchland." She shrugged again. "So far, not much magic has come up in my career, but this is one of those times when I have to wonder."

"Ah." Sarah sat back. "A lot happened up there." She struggled with how to tell the whole fantastic story, but she eventually succeeded, leaving out only a few things that felt too personal to share. They both hung on her every word, their mouths hanging open when she recounted the part about meeting with the ghosts in their glowing clearing.

Eli snapped his fingers. "I knew that deed was something more than a piece of paper. Anything to do with Lativia seems to have much more significance than at face value."

"Who could possibly want to remove the town's protection?" Jenna mused. "Doesn't seem very beneficial to anyone."

"And why murder Mr. Atticos? They could have just lured him outside . . . or knocked him out," Sarah also mused, sitting back in her chair heavily. It was then that she realized how sore her calves were from the hike.

Eli noticed her wince. "Are you okay?" he asked affectionately.

"*Oh, boy,*" Addie said in the background, where she sat near the window.

Sarah felt warm again under his smile. "I'm great, just sore from my hike," she replied a bit breathlessly. She turned to Jenna, who seemed slightly upset to see Eli's affectionate attention to Sarah.

"Couldn't you just recast the spell on a new document and protect the town all over again?" Jenna asked, hurriedly changing the subject.

"Possibly," Sarah said, liking the idea. "But I am not that powerful—yet, anyway. I still have a lot to learn. And Lativia wasn't very, uh, forthcoming with information. Honestly, if I could just get into her spellbook . . ."

"Maybe something relevant to this is locked in those pages." Eli nodded. "Interesting. She said music makes it work?"

"Yeah, whatever that means." Sarah sighed in frustration. "Why did she have to be annoyingly cryptic if she has all the answers?"

"Probably because she wants you to find them yourself," Jenna told her. "She's teaching you."

"Now seems like a bad time for a school lesson," Sarah scoffed. "The whole town is in jeopardy, and I'm not even equipped to handle it."

"Remember what she said about the wolf spirit? About how you're more like it than you think?" Eli asked.

Sarah nodded. She had left out the parts about seeing Michael again or about Michael and Addie turning into wolves. She wanted to keep that a secret, at least for now, until she knew what to do with the information. If Addie didn't want her to know right away, then the town cops didn't need to know, either. "Lativia says there are wolves in the forest again," she explained.

Jenna and Eli exchanged worried looks.

"That's not good. There were wolf prints and wolf fur on the clerk's body," Jenna reasoned. "Aggressive wolves could be a problem, and we can't have them hurting more villagers. If people find out that a wolf might have been behind this, they will go on a killing spree, and you know that wolves are protected by law."

"But if this were a simple mauling, it wouldn't be such a big case. Compounded with the robbery"—Eli shook his head—"it's not just some wolf attack."

"Could someone have trained a wolf to attack Mr. Atticos?" Jenna mused, her dark eyes dancing with intelligence as she mulled over the possible scenario.

"I highly doubt that," Sarah said uneasily, her first and foremost concern for the wolves in the forest. If people started killing wolves out of ignorance, thinking they were behind the murder, then she had double the work this time to save the forest.

How many murder mysteries combined with endangered species rescues do I have to solve here? she wondered with some exasperation and dismay.

"At least no one will think it's Addie," Jenna stated with authority.

Addie and Sarah both kept straight faces, but inside they were both screaming. "Wolves don't hunt people," Sarah started to explain. "They are more afraid of us than eager to attack us. After all, we've practically hunted them into extinction."

Jenna seemed dismissive. "If that's true, then that makes this case all the more suspicious that wild wolves are involved."

"I would encourage you to read up on wolves, Jenna," Sarah said, then changed the subject for now. "What did you get out of your interview with Mayor Lewis?"

Jenna widened her eyes. "Oh, he has my Spidey senses tingling, that's for sure."

"Very weird interview," Eli agreed. "I watched the tape and talked to him myself after Jenna, and we both were thrown off by his answers."

"His whole alibi was that he got some pizza from Geno's Ristorante Italiano and took it home. Watched old movies all night. Then went to bed around midnight. What's odd is that he signed out of the town hall around ten p.m. When I brought that up, he claimed he had forgotten to sign out and went back to sign out later. He saw the light on in Mr. Atticos's office and didn't think much of it," Jenna recounted.

"Anyway, I called Geno's, and they did sell him a pizza that night, but I don't think he went home to watch old movies until midnight because that's when his neighbors first saw his lights turn on." Jenna laid her hands on the table. "His body language was what really struck me as odd. Scratching his hair and ears, acting real nervous."

"Extremely fidgety," Eli agreed. "Like he had something to hide. He also had strange rashes on his body. He just seemed . . . like he had some strange illness."

"Illness?" Sarah was taken aback. "What could that be?"

"I don't know," Eli said, clearly concerned.

"And get this. When I asked him who might want the deed, his answer was, 'How should I know? It's not worth anything monetarily. And doesn't give anyone power over the town.' Though now that I know what the deed really does, I have to wonder how much he knew about that," Jenna went on.

"He seemed pretty resentful this morning about the deed. He said something about how he should have known about it, but didn't," Sarah recalled.

Eli nodded. "I remember that, too. Could it be he was stealing money, happened upon the deed, and took it just to empty out the safe? Maybe he has no intentions with it, no knowledge of it?" he theorized.

"I think I'll be paying him one more visit tomorrow." Jenna nodded. "Yep, definitely another visit."

"Now, I asked him if there's been a history of wild wolf attacks here, and that's when he said something really odd, something that makes me think he knows more about the magical side of Witchland than he's letting on," Eli piped up. "He acted perturbed by the question, as if it was a weird thing to ask, and then he said, 'There are no wolves here, but back in the day, people feared witches of the Wolf Coven. They claimed the witches could shapeshift into wolves and attack people. Witches could take the shapes of all kinds of animals.'"

Sarah cleared her throat, knowing this to be true. She glanced at Addie, who licked her chops and looked at her anxiously. Jenna twitched, that same intelligent light in her eyes, as she attempted to put two and two together.

Just then, Susie brought Sarah's sandwich. "We're closing soon, guys," Susie said gently. Then she froze, looking out the window, just as a ruckus started on the street. "What on earth is going on out there? Looks like a riot brewing."

A group of agitated people had gathered on the square in front of the coffee shop and apothecary. "Witch!" they were chanting. "Shapeshifter! Werewolf! Evil!"

Eli and Jenna bolted out of their chairs to rush outside. Sarah rushed after them.

"Hey! You're leaving behind perfectly good food!" Addie admonished them. But they weren't paying attention.

"What's going on?" Eli stormed up to the crowd.

"She killed Mr. Atticos!" a furious man pointed a shaky finger at the apothecary. "Like old times! That witch turned into a wolf and did it! They're all evil!"

"We need to clean them out, the witches!" shouted another woman whose face was beet red with anger.

"Calm down! Who are you talking about?" Jenna demanded.

"Daisy!" everyone shouted at once.

Sarah peered through the windows of the apothecary. She spotted Daisy, standing perfectly still behind her counter, watching the crowd outside with wide-eyed terror. An array of herbs were spread out before her. She had apparently been working all day, preparing for a peaceful evening at home, and now she was the center of a bitter protest against witches. Sarah felt horrible for her.

"There is absolutely no reason to assume Daisy did this," Eli admonished the crowd.

"Mayor Lewis told us it was her! He told us to watch out for these no-good witches!" a belligerent, red-faced man shouted back.

This might turn into a wolf hunt and *a witch hunt,* Sarah realized.

"You guys need to leave, before you all get tickets for disturbing the peace," Eli said firmly.

"Why don't you give her a ticket for being a

witch?" grumbled one of the men in the crowd as the people began to disperse begrudgingly. They kept looking over their shoulders at the apothecary, fear and hatred blazing in their eyes.

"This is not the 1600s," Eli shot back. "We don't have any laws in place to persecute witches, and especially not herbalists and small business owners."

Sarah shivered. While it was indeed chilly in the air, the vibes coming off of the townspeople were the true source of her discomfort. She sensed deep trouble brewing and a change in life as she knew it in Witchland.

"I can't believe there are such ignorant people in Witchland, of all places. You'd think everyone here would be tolerant of witchcraft," Jenna said, shaking her head in bewilderment.

"Let's go check on Daisy," Eli suggested.

Sarah nodded and followed him into the cozy apothecary. The strong fragrance of different herbs and spices filled her nostrils pleasantly. "Are you safe?" she asked, rushing to Daisy's side.

Daisy's hands trembled, but she appeared strong as she nodded. "I've always been delightfully welcome in this town, and now this. This reminds me of the old times, when religious fanatics would come to the apothecary my mother ran in Haiti and tell my mother and me that we were going to burn in Hell for what we were doing. Before that, when my parents migrated to the Dominican Republic to cut sugarcane, they were called dirty Haitians and deported back home. We've always been the victims of discrimination of all kinds." She managed a feeble, bittersweet smile. "Thanks for driving them away, Officers Eli Strongheart and Jenna Mora."

"I'm a bit concerned about your safety," Eli said. "Do you think you could stay in here, or at your house, until this blows over?"

Daisy reluctantly nodded. "I'm not closing up shop. Too many people need me. I'll just stay here, I guess."

"Keep the door locked, and don't let anyone but customers you know and trust inside," Eli cautioned.

"Do you think you need anything?" Sarah peered around the shop. Through a flimsy room divider, she could see a little room in the back with a cot and a small stove. "Seems like you have a place to lie down for the night."

"Oh, I'll be fine." Then Daisy shrugged. "I suppose I should get a few groceries to tide me over, and maybe a change of clothes from my house. A bar of soap." She laughed, attempting to lighten the mood, but it was clear she was still deeply unsettled. The worried furrow in her brow did not dissipate.

"I can get it all for you," Sarah offered.

Daisy handed her a key to her little cottage and a short grocery list, as well as a few crumpled bills. "No need to hurry. Go finish your food. I saw you guys in the café," Daisy urged her.

Sarah nodded. But as she, Jenna, and Eli stepped into the courtyard, Addie ran toward them, a torn shred of lettuce from Sarah's veggie sandwich protruding from between her black lips. *"Sorry! I thought you were going to waste it!"* Addie said when Sarah cried out her name.

Susie chased after her, breathless and red faced. "I tried to stop her from eating your food, but no such luck." She sighed exasperatedly. "Anyway, it's been a long day."

"I got the bill," Jenna informed them. When Eli and Sarah raised their voices to politely protest, she waved her hand dismissively. "Don't even worry about it. I need to go get some paperwork done and then go home. See you two later!" She nodded curtly at Sarah and waved goodbye to Eli before casting a final worried glance at the apothecary.

"Well, I guess I had better follow suit," Eli said. "You sure you don't need help?"

"Oh, I got it. I had better hurry, though. The grocer is closing any minute now." Everyone in Witchland was sure to rise before the sun, but they didn't stay open very late past dark.

Eli gave her an apologetic smile. "Well, thanks for all of your help. Sorry . . . about all of this." He waved in the direction of the courtyard, referring to the ruckus of earlier. "It's really not very fair to people like you. You witches really just try to help. And after all that Daisy has done for people, well, it's just sad."

"No, it's not fair. Daisy is a really wonderful person." Sarah didn't want to see Eli leave, but she had to say goodbye quickly and hurried to the grocer's with Addie. She looked forward to seeing him tomorrow. She kept thinking about how cute he looked as he apologized for the discrimination her magically inclined kind faced. How empathetic and kind he was! What a man!

"*Thinking about Prince Charming?*" Addie teased as they entered the grocer's.

"Stay out of my head." Sarah laughed.

"*Honestly, I'm still thinking about food.*" Addie licked her chops and sniffed the air as she trotted behind Sarah.

The grocer's was an old-fashioned market, with racks of fresh meat hanging from the ceiling and fresh seafood lined neatly in ice in the case at the butcher's counter, and huge loaves of crusty bread cooling in racks in the bakery. Large bins of produce still crusted with dirt from local farms and gardens crowded the middle of the store. Snacks, grains, beans, nuts, and candies were sold in bulk in large glass containers lining the haphazard rows. The smell of meat, fish, vegetables, and fruit was almost repulsive, yet also mouth-watering. It reminded Sarah of the farmer's market and fish market in New York, but it smelled even fresher and more wholesome.

"I am, too. I wouldn't be so hungry if *someone* hadn't eaten my sandwich!" Sarah grumbled.

"You can get us steaks," Addie urged. *"You know, to make up for the sandwich."*

"You don't deserve a steak right now, and you know I don't eat meat." Sarah shook her head, both irritated and amused by her dog at the moment. Her stomach grumbled.

She groaned internally when she spotted a pointy black hat over the top of one of the shelves, advancing in her direction. Harriet appeared, her pet crow roosted on her shoulder. "Ah, Ms. Spellwood! What happened to the Jimmy shoes and the smoky eyes?" She cackled.

Sarah had not even thought about applying makeup for several weeks, and her Jimmy Choo high heels were collecting dust in her narrow bedroom closet. She had been thinking about donating them, to make space for things she actually needed. But Harriet's constant cracks about her spiffy clothes and makeup annoyed her to no end.

"Hi, Harriet," she said, forcing politeness. "You might want to watch out, walking around town in that witch getup. People are getting upset and accusing witches of shapeshifting and murdering the town clerk."

Harriet merely snorted. "How about I give them all a shot of fermented toad liver juice with chamomile and valerian and calm them all right down? They know my bird is trained to kill, anyway. Huh, isn't that right, Edgar?" She stroked her crow's beak.

The crow flapped its wings merrily and danced up and down on her bony shoulder. It let out a single croak, attracting amused glances from a couple, who were obviously tourists visiting the town, browsing through the barrel of broccoli heads.

Sarah suppressed a shudder and a gag at the mention of fermented toad liver juice and began to walk away. "Okay, well, just be careful," she said.

"You be careful," Harriet responded. "You have some proving to do yourself before we can honestly say if you're good or if you're evil!" Then she bobbed out of the store, not purchasing anything, cackling to herself as if she had just told a hilarious joke.

Sarah felt perplexed, then she rolled her eyes.

"Whatever. I can't put too much stock in what that crazy lady has to say. I can't believe she would say that after all that I tried to do for the town and the lynx. Must be nothing to it."

"You might want to listen to her," Addie replied sagely. *"There is a Native American belief that we all have two wolves in us, one good and one evil. The one we choose to feed is the one who grows the strongest. That saying is especially true for women of the Wolf Coven. Remember, Madras is of the same bloodline and the same magical background as Lativia!"*

Sarah felt chilled again at the mention of Madras. "You are right, Addie, there's good and bad in all of us. But I feed my good wolf. And now I'd really like to feed it, literally. Come on let's get some food for us and also get Daisy's shopping done."

As she browsed the aisles for some of the simple things Daisy had scrawled on the list, such as white beans and rice, she noticed two men in grubby camouflage flannel and dirty hiking boots standing an aisle over. They were browsing cans of beans. The clerk was staying open just for them and for Sarah, though she looked none too pleased about it.

"I'm telling you, it's that dang wolf we saw the other day," one man was saying in a hushed voice.

"He was a big monster," the other agreed solemnly.

"They said the body had wolf prints on it. And bits

of gray fur. That wolf we saw is gray!" the first hunter went on.

Sarah and Addie exchanged scared looks. Indeed, witches and wolves both were threatened now. "We have to find this wolf," Sarah told Addie.

"No *kidding*," Addie said. *"Before he gets shot or something."*

"I am supposed to help the wolves, aren't I? That's what she meant by being their protector?" Suddenly, Lativia's message on Mount Katribus was starting to make a bit more sense. Her deliberate vagueness was starting to become clear. Sarah grinned, happy her current purpose was finally illuminated. "It's like with the lynx. I have to protect and save all of the animals in these woods from ill-intentioned humans."

Addie barked in happy agreement and wagged her tail.

CHAPTER SIX

Sarah bolted back to the Mount Katribus trailhead, eager to find out more about the wolf and how to protect him, but a firefighter stopped her. "Fire up there," he said. "Forest fire. Were you up there recently?"

Sarah stared up at the mountain. Sure enough, there was a fire, with black smoke billowing above the trees. Thankfully, it wasn't spreading. Sarah felt her chest tighten with grief for Clover Figcreek and the Leekins, the wolves, and all of the other creatures she was meant to protect. Who knew how many lives were being lost as the flames consumed the trees?

Suddenly, she was able to identify the sick feeling of unease that had been brewing in her stomach since the coffee shop. It was the presence of evil.

Sarah mumbled something unintelligible to the

firefighter, who was staring at her as if she was possessed, and hurried off to the apothecary. Halfway there, she realized she had run out of the grocery without grabbing any of Daisy's items. "Oh, no!" she cried out loud, immediately changing course back to her house. She found some rice and beans in her cupboards, and grabbed a bar of soap. Then she ran a jagged path to Daisy's cottage, which was near Harriet's oddly-shaped hut, and grabbed everything Daisy required there. The incense scent in Daisy's cottage was pleasantly intoxicating and made Sarah want to simply collapse into Daisy's massive, silk-dressed bed. *I am so tired and out of breath already, and running in the cold is not fun!* she thought. *But there's no rest when you are a sworn protector of the forest, I guess.*

Her arms were laden with things as she hastened to the apothecary. Then it occurred to her what she must do. She must crack the code and read her ancestor's book! Lativia's spellbook surely held some answers about how to stop this. Some fire-stopping spell, perhaps, or a protective spell for the forest. She had to get home and figure out the music thing and get into that book! After this errand, she resolved to crack into the book, once and for all.

Strangely, a man Sarah didn't recognize was in the apothecary by the time she arrived. He appeared very tall, with thick, dark hair. He was yelling, "How can you put this whole town in danger with your evil magic? We all know about you! And what you do!" He waved a disparaging arm at Daisy's vast array of pills, powders, and elixirs in colorful glass bottles with hand-written labels.

Daisy shrunk even farther from him. Her face was drawn taut, and her eyes were brimming with tears. Sarah had never seen the spunky, spirited woman look so small, not even when the mob had been protesting her shop an hour ago.

At the sight of him, Addie raised her hackles and growled. The man wheeled around, his face flushed and his breath rapid. Sarah found something vaguely familiar about his face, though she still could not place him just yet.

"Is there a problem here?" Sarah asked. The man scared her, but she had to draw strength from her heart, her ancestors, and her new duty as the protector of the forest as well as the wolves.

"Yeah, there's a big problem! This friend here of yours? She's poisoning the town with gosh knows what. And on top of that, she's a werewolf!" he bellowed. "She probably murdered that poor clerk, or drove somebody to it. We all know she's making people crazy with her weird potions and brews. Heck, she's why John is the violent maniac he's become! He wasn't like that before! I know my brother!" He shook his fist in the air for emphasis.

Addie began to slowly approach him, a low growl emerging from deep in her throat. His eyes widened as he backed away, raising his hands. "Get that mongrel under control," he said, but his voice lacked its former toughness.

"I'm sorry, but who are you?" Sarah demanded, crossing her arms. It was one thing to insult magic, but to insult Addie was too much for Sarah to tolerate. She took insults to Addie, her familiar, as personal insults to herself.

"Levi Gonforth," the man replied, nervously glancing at Addie and then at Sarah. His voice now trembled. "John's brother."

Now Sarah realized why he looked so familiar. He was the brother of the real estate attorney and Michael's rival, who had nearly killed her with morphine just a month ago and tried to make it look like a freak accident. She still struggled with the painful memory of what had happened in the doctor's office when John and Dismas had attempted to take her life. At times, she had nightmares about the crooks' faces. Now John was in prison, and his brother was in town, seeking revenge. He looked a bit like John, though he had his own unique striking features, and he was clearly enraged.

"Well, Levi, I'm sorry about your brother. But you're actually committing the act of harassment right now, and I have to ask you to leave." Sarah gestured for Addie to follow her and strode past Levi, placing Daisy's necessities on the apothecary counter. "If you don't leave right now, I will have to call the police and have you arrested for trespassing." She pointed at the sign hanging over the door, 'Closed' written on it in white chalk.

He gulped as recognition spread across his face. "You're that new lawyer, aren't you? The one who accused my brother of trying to murder you?"

"Yep, I sure am." Sarah stood up tall and faced him, as desperately as she wanted to shrink away.

"I know my brother, you liar. He never would have done that. You just wanted him out of the picture because you knew he was a million times better at law than you!" Levi bellowed.

"He did try to kill me, and one thing I'm sure of is that I am a darn good attorney. I know the law inside and out. Now, you have one second to turn around and leave," Sarah replied in her firmest tone.

The man glanced from her to Daisy, then swallowed and began to back out of the store. "You poisoned my brother!" he shouted a final time as his hand located the door latch behind his back.

"Daisy had nothing to do with what John did. John

made a choice to do what he did in the name of greed," Sarah replied. "If you want to keep leveling accusations, I suggest you take it up with Officer Eli Strongheart."

"I think I will!" Levi cried tremulously, already halfway out the door. He shot Sarah, Daisy, and then Addie one last terrified look before bolting. Though he was trying to be tough, his veneer was rapidly wearing off in the face of Sarah's toughness.

"Are you okay?" Sarah rubbed Daisy's elbow.

Daisy nodded and swallowed. "I had no idea people thought such bad things about me. I really thought this town was . . . home. A place where I was accepted and welcomed." She blinked, and a tear spilled down her cheek. "Anyway, witches don't cry." She turned to a small Bunsen burner, over which she was heating a flask filled with a strange red liquid.

"Well, I have your things here. I'm sorry it took me so long. Where do you want them?" Sarah asked, her heart still hammering from the unpleasant encounter with Levi Gonforth.

"Just set them on the counter. You've done so much for me. Thank you."

Sarah smiled. "It's my pleasure. I can't stand by and let you be bullied and harassed, especially over something that you had absolutely nothing to do with."

"I would do anything for you, too," Daisy replied. "You're Beth's niece! You're family to me."

"Actually, there is a favor you could do for me right now, if you can," Sarah said suddenly as an idea occurred to her.

"What do you need?" Daisy blinked at her, attempting a feeble smile. She was always ready to set her own problems aside and assist, like a true healer.

"I am about to go home and crack open Lativia's book. But I also need a book on paranormal law, if you have it. I think I'll need it to do my job. Which, by the way, Lativia told me is protecting wolves and the forest as a whole," Sarah said proudly, trying not to give away her anxiety about her abilities to accomplish all her ancestor expected of her.

Daisy smiled genuinely this time. "I had a sense that is what Lativia intended for you. She wanted her family to take over her job of town protector so that she could finally fully transition to the afterlife. Well, I'm sure you will do a wonderful job." She seemed to genuinely mean it, and Sarah felt reassured.

Daisy began to go through some books she kept in a small, shelved room behind the front part of the shop. "I know I have a great book. I just have to find it."

"Thank you, but I have no clue how to proceed with all of this. Lativia told me music unlocks her spellbook."

Daisy paused, her face lighting up. "How fascinating! I never thought of that. Old spells read like songs, so that makes perfect sense."

"I still don't know how to proceed, though. Do I just play it music? And what kind of music?" Sarah wondered.

Daisy smiled and suggested, "Just experiment with different genres! Maybe sing to the book. Play an instrument."

"Well, while I experiment with the music, I think understanding the laws of magic can also be . . . helpful. At least, in this case." Sarah followed Daisy and ran her fingers over the spines of ancient, dusty volumes, many of which had titles she could not understand.

"Of course! Laws of magic are always important," Daisy replied. "Even the world of magic is governed by rules. Not following them . . . well, that's never good." She located a particularly dense volume, and Sarah sighed as Daisy placed it in her hands.

"Reminds me of law school all over again," she joked.

"Yes, that should take you a few years to read." Daisy laughed. She returned to her potion on the tiny burner while tucking her dreadlocks into her orange silk scarf. "Well, my dear, I have had quite a day, and I would like to get some rest. You have been so kind—if there is ever anything else I can help you with, feel free to call on me."

Sarah hugged her, and then urged her to lock the apothecary door as she left with Addie trotting at her side.

"I'm glad I don't have to read that," Addie said about the book in Sarah's arms, which she had to carry like a baby due to its humongous bulk.

The next morning, after a particularly restless night, Sarah headed to the police station. She was disappointed not to see Officer Eli at his desk, and Jenna informed her that he was helping an elderly lady whose cat had run up into a tree. "Finkles usually takes a few hours to be coaxed out, so try back around noon?" Jenna suggested, sipping from a steaming mug of coffee.

"Well, actually, you can help me just as much as Eli can," Sarah replied.

"Oh? Well, take a seat." Jenna indicated the chair in front of her cluttered desk. "What's up?"

Sarah repeated what she had heard the hunters say in the store the night before. "I feel that wolves may be in danger, like we talked about yesterday, and they may not even be the perpetrator. With everyone pointing fingers at wild wolves or Daisy, they are making it easier for the true perp to hide," Sarah concluded.

Jenna nodded. "Of course. I must say, there have been no reports of wolf attacks or even sightings around Witchland. It makes me wonder about this even more. And I did some research and saw you were right, actually. The likelihood of a lone wolf attacking a human is low. And one attacking a grown man in a fairly populated area with some vehicle traffic and lights nearby? Pretty much impossible. Wolves may attack if they are rabid, of course—but there have been no reports of rabies in this area. Ever. I already checked with Fish and Game."

"Excellent. Do you agree that I should probably find this wolf that the hunters saw? And try to talk to him?" Sarah was excited, knowing that Eli and Jenna both were open-minded about magic and knowledge-able of the true nature of Witchland.

But what Jenna said next absolutely threw her for a loop.

Jenna nodded slowly. "Of course. Whatever you think would help. But I must admit, this has me worried. See"—she paused, looking Sarah up and down—"I have to tell you something that I couldn't really say in front of Eli yesterday because, well, I'm not sure he's ready to hear it. He's not from here originally; we're lucky he accepts that the Leekins and magic are real."

Sarah scooted to the end of her seat, hanging on Jenna's every word. "Yes?" she prodded. She had gotten the sense that Jenna did not particularly care for her, so she was pleasantly surprised that Jenna wanted to confide something to her that she couldn't even confide to her partner.

Jenna breathed out heavily. "I'm not just a cop. I'm a protector of Witchland, too. I'm a paranormal gatekeeper."

Sarah felt her mouth fall open. Jenna, who seemed like the most nonmagical, straight-laced person on the planet, was involved in the paranormal herself! "Wait, what's a gatekeeper? You're a witch?" Her eyes scanned Jenna's face, her pressed dark blue uniform, her neat and undecorated office.

"I don't practice magic, per se. Not the way you are trying to, or the way Daisy or Hua and Margaret do." Jenna leaned forward, folding her hands on the desk. "My job is to protect this town from evil and enforce the laws that Lativia put in place to guard this place from evil—namely, Madras.

"You already know that Lativia and others in her coven are wolf power spirits. What you don't know is that Madras is, too. She was a part of the same coven at one point. As she began to delve into dark magic, the coven tried to intervene, but Madras got drunk on power. Greed does that to people; that's why people fall to the dark side, and don't even realize they are evil. Sadly, that's what happened to Madras, and when she was caught possessing magic books, she was sentenced to be burned at the stake. Lativia was, too, because she was obviously a witch as well. Always healing people with herbs, talking to animals. Both witches were sentenced to be burned on the same day, and they both could have been saved by their coven. But only Lativia was saved.

"You see, Lativia was beaten and very weak—she couldn't save herself. But when her coven members showed up as a pack of wolves, scaring the crowd and her executioner away, she found the strength to turn into a wolf again, and she slid out of her bonds. That's how we're all here today, practicing her magic. But the coven could not save Madras because she was too far gone into the darkness. She refused their help and tried to summon the help of a demon instead. She thought dark magic was better, stronger. Pride got the best of her. Well, that choice backfired on her because the demon she summoned let her burn in order to gain full control of her soul.

"Even in death, Madras remained a powerful force of magic, now that she was half demon. She gained more and more power after death, in fact, aided by all of the dark spirits that aligned themselves with her ghost, making her more and more demonic. As she became more powerful, she also became more furious. Her power spirit started to look less like a wolf and more like a demon in wolf shape, and she began to stay in that shape most of the time, instead of looking like her former human self. For years, she stalked the woods, seeking her revenge on her former sisters who had abandoned her to die and the people who burned her at the stake. She is the reason there are so many legends about wolf witches killing people in the woods, and why wolves are particularly feared and hated here. Lativia had to put a stop to Madras killing people, so she became especially committed to protecting both wolves and people from her sister.

"I can't say this in any official police report, but I think maybe a wolf *did* kill Mr. Atticos. But it wasn't some wild wolf. I think it could be Madras, back at her old tricks. Part of my job is to protect this town from her and her forces, to enforce the paranormal law and ensure that no one breaks it. That's how Witchland has remained a safe place for so long. I did not know about the deed's protective spell, but I guess that's why my job has been pretty easy. Now with the deed gone, I fear that Madras is lurking, able to get in finally." Jenna sighed as she sat back in her chair. "This is not good, Sarah, not good at all. And I think you're supposed to help us find Madras and put an end to her wicked ways, while also protecting innocent wolves."

Sarah took a deep breath. "This all makes so much sense," she said, gradually expelling the air from deep in her lungs. "Honestly, I don't know where to begin, but I already decided to start studying paranormal law to know what I'm dealing with."

"Good start. Now go find that wolf, and let me know how it goes." Jenna gave her an encouraging smile. "There are donuts, by the way."

Sarah appreciated this new gesture of friendship and the sense that Jenna was setting aside her jealousy to work with Sarah on their common goal of defending Witchland from evil forces. Though she felt bad about it, she had to decline. "I'm not hungry, but thanks. I really need to get around that firefighter and go find this wolf—or wolves—before they get confused with Madras's wolf. And maybe they can tell me if they saw anything like a demon wolf hanging around. Maybe one of them even witnessed the crime."

"Go find your wolf," Jenna agreed, while Addie scolded Sarah in dismay for not eating.

As Sarah began to jog down the street toward the Mount Katribus trailhead, she passed the grocer's. Levi Gonforth was coming out, empty-handed. He stopped and stared at her, a hostile expression on his face.

"*I don't like how he looks at you,*" Addie said protectively.

"Me neither," Sarah muttered nervously. "But we

can't worry about him right now."

"That's right! We have a job to do," Addie agreed.

"It's odd he's here right when Madras appears to be lurking around, but I am not sure if it's just a coincidence or not. Do you think he could be somehow helping her out?" Sarah mused.

"I certainly don't like the feeling I get from him," Addie noted.

The firefighter was at his post at the trailhead once again. He glared at Sarah suspiciously as she smiled innocently at him. She pretended she was merely going for a walk with Addie as she turned back toward her house and snuck into the woods from her backyard. There were no trails, but Addie promised, *"I can already smell the wolf, I'll track him and keep us from getting lost."*

Once in the privacy and gloom of the trees, Addie began to morph into her wolf form so that she could smell more accurately and also earn the trust of any wolves they discovered. Sarah watched the process, still finding it both entrancing and slightly bizarre as Addie grew broad, sleek, and sharp-looking.

Sarah remembered the spell Hua had taught her and became one with the trees, camouflaging herself from anyone who might interrupt them. It felt nice to become one with the solitary, deep-rooted serenity of the trees, with their ancient wisdom and silent observations. She added the spell to include Addie. This way only she and the wolf they were tracking could see her. The last thing she wanted was some trigger-happy hunter or some person like Levi Gonforth seeing Addie and killing her for the murder of the town clerk.

Addie put her nose to the ground, and they began to track.

"Do you smell anything?" Sarah asked after what seemed to be a really long time of Addie vigorously sniffing random plants and tree roots.

"Oh, yeah. His pee stinks!" she replied. *"He's been here. Probably this morning."*

"He? Addie, you just smell one?" Sarah urged her for more information.

"Yes, just one so far. He's a lone wolf," Addie said, a strange tone of admiration in her voice.

"Well, where is he now?" Sarah peered through the trees. The woods were eerily quiet, without the usual bird chatter; the scent of woodsmoke added to the ominous sense that something was very, very wrong.

"I'm trying to find that out! Just be patient!" Addie replied. *"The trail is getting stronger...."*

"I heard you were looking for me?" A deep, slightly sardonic voice startled Sarah.

Addie looked up from her scent trail and froze. *"Oh my wagging tail, he's . . . huge,"* she gasped to Sarah.

Sarah could tell he was beautiful, at least by human standards. There were red and yellow notes to his thick, silver fur and his yellow eyes were laser focused on them as his ears pointed forward, listening. He was much larger than Addie, even in her wolf form. Though Sarah wanted to trust him, since he was her spirit animal after all, she also felt uneasy being so near an obviously wild creature.

"Hello." Addie wagged her tail as she approached him slowly. *"We needed to talk to you."*

"I'm listening." He sat on his haunches, looking at them expectantly.

"Uh . . . well . . ." Addie looked to Sarah for help. Sarah had never seen her this flustered and shy before.

"I just need to know one thing. Did you kill Mr. Atticos?" Sarah asked, trying to stand her ground and keep the shakiness from her voice. She sensed that in order to effectively talk to wolves, she had to think like them. Since wolves operated on a pack mentality, respecting the most alpha member of the pack, she knew that she had to earn this wolf's respect with a dominant posture and firm voice.

The wolf laughed. *"A human? Why would I kill a human? I'm a real wolf! I much prefer the taste of the wild beasts that roam these here woods or, when I'm lazy, Mrs. Roth's chickens, honestly."*

"Those chickens do smell good," Addie agreed,

longing in her voice. She was too well behaved to ever attack other animals, particularly domesticated ones, but the urges clearly remained in her instincts.

"Try them first thing in the morning," the wolf told her. *"The taste of hot blood . . ."*

"Okay. Okay," Sarah interjected impatiently, this talk about killing animals and eating meat making her feel sick to her stomach. "We're not here to talk about food, Mr. Wolf. Did you happen to see his murder take place?"

"I wasn't watching," he responded, a touch of laziness in his voice. *"I don't concern myself with the silliness of humans too much. I like the solitariness of my forest, the fairness and order of nature."*

"I need you to listen to me and really pay attention." Sarah leaned toward him, noticing the massive power of his muscular haunches. "As you know, humans aren't always very fair or orderly."

The wolf turned to her, a twinkle of respect in his eye. He was starting to appear less haughty and more submissive in his body language. *"Okay?"*

"That's why you are in a lot of danger. People think you killed Mr. Atticos. Or they think you're a witch, turned into a wolf. You have to be careful," she warned.

The wolf tilted his head to the side. *"How could they confuse me with the dark and humongous wolf?*

My, I wish humans would work on their scent skills. I smell and look nothing like her, and I'm also the real deal, one hundred percent raw wolf."

Addie let out a small sigh, as if she were about to swoon.

Sarah froze. "You've seen the Madras demon wolf? As in, you've actually seen her with your eyes?"

"Ugly scarred wolf with red eyes like fire, eating my rabbits, marking my trees. Of course. Why do you think the mountain is falling apart?" The wolf indicated the summit with his nose, where the fire now raged, the stink of its smoke floating to where they were standing. *"That demon wolf is here destroying the whole ecosystem."*

Sarah was speechless. Jenna was right! Madras was already here, harming Witchland! That did not take Madras very long at all to start trouble after stealing the deed.

"I just worry someone might shoot you, thinking you're Madras." Sarah sighed. "Please take care of yourself."

"Of course. Don't worry about me. If you need anything, your familiar here can find me." He glanced at Addie, who was giving him a simpering look of longing. *"I definitely would not object to seeing you again. But bring me one of those bones your witch gives you to gnaw on that I've seen littering your yard."*

"*I will,*" Addie said adoringly, her voice sounding very far away.

"*The name is Kelvin,*" he added.

"*Kelvin,*" she repeated in a soft murmur.

Addie seemed distracted as they returned to town.

Sarah felt panic rising in her chest, elevating her blood pressure. *Madras! This powerful dark witch is here, and I have to fight her, and I am only a novice!* "Stop being afraid," she told herself aloud. "I'm a Spellwood. I'm a powerful witch. At one point I was just a law student, and I won my first case against those nasty creeps trying to tear down a historic hotel in Manhattan!" Confidence began to blossom in her heart, chasing away the fear. "Yeah, I can do this. I can do this!"

As she psyched herself up to Addie, Addie only replied with the occasional foggy, "*Uh-huh.*"

"Are you even listening?" Sarah finally demanded.

"*Sorry, can't help it,*" Addie said, shaking her head. "*Did you hear him? He wants to see me again.*"

Sarah realized that this must be how she acted whenever she left a meeting with Eli. Her heart melted. "I'm glad you found someone," she teased affectionately, watching Addie shed her wolf form and become an innocent-looking golden mixed-breed collie again.

CHAPTER SEVEN

Sarah paused for a second to rub her eyes; they felt grainy from reading the dense, stilted language of the paranormal law book, which was printed in the tiniest font size possible, on the most yellowed and water-damaged pages Sarah had ever seen. She was attempting to make some sort of sense of the mire of words about how gatekeepers worked, about their role keeping Madras and other dark spirits at bay through a complex network of daily spells and hexes and incantations. A gatekeeper's job seemed to consist mostly of watching for warning signs of impending danger while also frequently replenishing the power behind any protective spells that may have been placed over an area. Jenna's job was doubly important now that Lativia was dead, though Lativia still managed to have fairly significant magical influence, from what Sarah could tell. Sarah enjoyed learning about what Jenna really did besides regular law enforcement. Sarah certainly would not have guessed her secret magical identity if Jenna had not confided in her and handed her the answer to who was causing trouble in the forest.

Eager for a break, Sarah was glad when Eli texted her, inviting her to meet him for coffee at Javacadabra. Of course, she was glad to see Eli anytime.

"You're just using a need for fresh air and coffee as an excuse to see Eli," Addie teased her. *"You wouldn't take a break earlier when I told you to."*

"Yeah, yeah, and you keep trying to run off into the forest to see Kelvin any chance you get, so you have no right to talk," Sarah teased back.

Arriving at the coffee shop, Sarah felt her usual rush when she saw Eli, handsome as ever in his uniform. She was also glad to see he was alone. He grinned and waved her to the table. "I already got you your usual," he told her, handing her a green tea latte.

Sarah breathed in the fragrant steam off her beverage. "Mmm, delightful. That's so sweet you remembered what I always order."

Eli looked down to hide his slight blush. "Well, of course."

"John Gonforth's brother is in town," Sarah

crowed, feeling proud to be able to offer some new intel.

But Eli nodded grimly, already well aware of the new menace. "He is my suspect number one, I can tell you that much. And Daisy is number nine billion—despite what the town thinks."

Sarah hesitated. "Have you spoken to Jenna about . . . about her theory? About someone, er, using a wolf form or a trained wolf?" She had to keep Jenna's secret, so she didn't let on she knew about Jenna's suspicions about Madras.

But apparently Eli knew about that, too. He sighed impatiently. "Jenna kind of hinted about it to me, that she thinks there's dark magic involved and maybe Madras has returned to duel with Lativia again. She's possibly right. It's happened before in the history of this town. But none of it makes sense in this case, though."

"Why not?" Sarah asked.

"Think about it. If Madras was barred from the town, how could she have gotten in to commit the murder and *then* make away with the deed? Something tells me that someone else was involved, someone who wants to see this town fall. Someone let Madras in and killed the clerk—and who would have the motive to do that?"

"Levi Gonforth," Sarah realized. "Oh, no! It makes

so much sense. He's mad his brother couldn't take over the forest, therefore he did what he could to see Witchland crumble anyway."

"Absolutely. But there is no evidence to tie him to the crime as of this moment. Honestly, I think he framed Mayor Lewis, and he sure did a great job of it. Because Mayor Lewis would look super guilty to a jury, and Levi would look squeaky clean. Mayor Lewis was there that night at the town hall, he has been missing work ever since, and he doesn't have an alibi. Levi? Can't be placed near the scene of the crime. I can't exactly take him off the streets now, but who knows what else he is capable of." Eli ground his jaw, and Sarah realized how anxious and tense he was over this crime.

"Do you have any news about the fire?" She sipped her tea latte, hoping her own headache and eyestrain would dissipate. She was as tense and anxious as Eli, if not more so. The idea of somehow going up against Madras was weighing on her quite heavily.

"It won't extend past the peak of Mount Katribus. The firefighters can't figure out a source," Eli informed her.

"The peak . . . where Lativia and the ghosts are. And Kelvin told me about a new wolf, a demon wolf," Sarah mused out loud.

Eli peered at her. "Kelvin?"

Addie perked up at the sound of his name. *"Kelvin?"* she also repeated.

"A wolf I met in the woods. It doesn't matter," Sarah said.

"You met a real wolf and you don't think it matters? Sarah!" Eli admonished. "That wolf could be instrumental to solving this crime. What if he was, you know, involved somehow?"

"He's not," Sarah assured him.

"And how do you know that for an absolute fact?" Eli took on a slightly patronizing tone that irritated Sarah.

"I have intuition," Sarah sputtered, realizing how weak her argument sounded. It would definitely flop in front of a jury! "Look, I really do think Madras is here! Kelvin has seen her, and you said yourself she has a history of battling Lativia for control of this town and forest." Sarah pounded the table with her fist in excitement. "And from what I've been told, I think the forest fire is caused by her, as well as the murder. She's at the peak, because Lativia is there. From what Jenna told me, they're an even match now as far as supernatural powers go. And I think I have to go to the peak and battle her! I have to intervene or Madras might even win!"

"That's interesting, how do you win?" Eli said

skeptically, clearly as alarmed as Sarah was about the prospect of a battle with Madras.

"I have no idea, but I think Lativia's spellbook could help. She told me it likes music, so I have to find a tune to unlock its words." Sarah leaned forward and began to rub her temples. "So far I've tried several kinds of music with no luck. I've even sang to it—and I can't sing! I have such a bad headache from trying to sort all of this stuff out!"

Eli leaned forward and rubbed her shoulder, clearly concerned. "I don't want you wearing yourself out and then trying to face a powerful dark witch. After all, you really need to be at your best for this."

Sarah felt tears spring into her tears. It had been a long time since she had cried, but she couldn't help it now. "I'm scared," she whispered.

Eli looked pained as he wrapped a protective arm around her shoulders. "I know you are. I am, too. But the both of us have to be brave. This is our duty in life, to protect innocent people and animals. Sarah, we are here to make the world a better place." He glanced at Addie, who was appraising him approvingly.

"I know. And I wouldn't trade any of this for my old life in New York. But sometimes, I wonder just what the heck I got myself into!" Sarah hastily wiped away her tears but didn't try to shrug off Eli's arm around her. When he didn't remove his arm, she felt warm and pleased. His muscles were delightfully firm.

"I came here for some peace and quiet myself, but we sure didn't get that here, did we?" Eli laughed kindly. "I was a cop in Buffalo, and saw some pretty awful stuff. Stuff I still see in my nightmares. Then my divorce . . . well, it broke me inside. I had nothing to live for anymore. When I saw an opening at the police department here, I decided I needed a change of pace, that I deserved some beauty and stillness in my life. Hiking and kayaking on my days off, rescuing cats out of trees, friendly folks who say hi, and the grandmas of the town who bring me homemade brownies."

Sarah turned to survey his face, shocked at how much they shared in common. "I went through a pretty brutal divorce myself." She laughed bittersweetly. "I also didn't have much of a life in New York anymore, so I felt that Michael was guiding me to my destiny when he left me his house and law practice. I didn't know you went through something similar to that, too."

Eli looked away for a second before meeting her eyes again. "It's hard to talk about, but my ex-wife had an affair with my partner, actually. That's why I really like having Jenna as a partner. She would never do something like that! Loyalty is very important in life and especially in law enforcement, and you take it for granted until you've been stabbed in the back."

"I think Jenna wants to work with me and to be my ally, but I sense she also views me as a threat," Sarah reticently disclosed.

"A threat? A threat in what way?" Eli seemed baffled.

"I think Jenna likes you," Sarah informed him shyly. "As more than just a cop partner."

Eli widened his eyes and recoiled slightly. "Oh, no, we're strictly professional. There's absolutely nothing romantic between us. Never has been."

"That doesn't mean she doesn't like you," Sarah said softly.

"I'm not here looking for love," Eli said suddenly and curtly, pulling his arm away from around Sarah's shoulders. "Been there, done that."

Sarah felt stung. The last thing she had wanted to do was make Eli mad, or create awkwardness between them! This last bit of news discouraged her, as she had just begun to think he might be into her. Then again, dating had never been her strong suit, and besides Jeff, she had had only one boyfriend in high school. She could understand long spells and complicated tort law, but reading the signs of men boggled her mind. Maybe she had read Eli wrongly.

Eli seemed to read her hurt and promptly softened, leaning toward her again. "I tell you what. How about you work on unlocking the spellbook today, and I'll work on getting some info on Levi's whereabouts the night Mr. Atticos was killed?"

Sarah nodded, wondering if she could get into the frame of mind she needed to be in to work on the spellbook now. She could envision herself overthinking what Eli had said all afternoon!

"If we stay busy and ahead of this mess, the fear won't get to us as badly. That's how I learned to confront fear in my police training."

"Sounds good," Sarah agreed.

Back home, Sarah laid open Lativia's spellbook and played a few different songs. Nothing happened. Frustrated, she slammed the book closed. "Why can't you just tell me how to do this, Lativia?" she wailed, knowing that Lativia's ghost could probably hear her.

As night fell, Sarah felt the itch to do some investigating that only she could do with her powers and the spells she now knew. She decided to go on the prowl, like a wolf, and use the camouflaging spell to see if she could unearth more about the suspects in the murder. Maybe she could even find some suspects of her own!

While so far she had only used the camouflage spell to hide among trees, she wondered if she might be able to use it with other plants and even objects like stone walls. After all, even nonliving things had spirits and essences that she could use to mesh with, as Hua and Margaret had taught her.

She practiced for a while and realized that her theory worked. By taking in the essence of both animate and inanimate objects, she could blend in with them seamlessly. She experimented by prancing around the town square; when no one seemed to look at her or greet her, she began to make silly faces. Still no one responded. She knew she must be invisible to them!

Now she was prepared to stalk her suspects and find out more than Eli could legally. *Maybe Lativia was wrong. I have actually learned something very useful from Hua and Margaret!* she thought.

Singing "Hungry Like the Wolf" by Duran Duran under her breath, she dressed warmly in preparation for the frigid night. "Am I wrong for spying on people? Isn't that what they want my help with, saving the town from evil and criminals?" she asked Addie. "I'm not always sure how to do my job as protector of the forest because everyone has been uncomfortably vague. I can't tell what's wrong or right at this time. Currently, this is the only way I can think of to get things done."

Addie had been dreamy since the meeting with Kelvin, and it took her a second to catch up with what

Sarah was saying. *"Yeah, of course,"* she said dismissively.

"I really need you to focus," Sarah remonstrated. "After all, you're always telling me not to get too distracted by Eli!"

"Uh-huh," Addie said absentmindedly.

Sarah was particularly interested in the activities of Levi Gonforth, who certainly had motive to take over the town as his brother had originally intended. She was also interested in Mayor Lewis, who had been calling in sick to the town hall meetings and avoiding his office every day since the murder, according to Eli. While she already knew Daisy was not to blame, she decided to visit the apothecary first, in an attempt to exonerate her.

But before she left home with Addie, Sarah pulled her close, took a deep breath, and smiled at her canine companion. "Here we go, Addie!" she said before chanting:

> *Make us invisible*
> *And cloak us by our oath.*
> *We will reveal the divisible*
> *For information's growth!*

Daisy had not left her apothecary in the past two days. Wearing the same clothes and orange silk head scarf as the days before, she stood behind her counter, stirring that same red potion. Sarah, fully invisible, noticed how strong it smelled.

Suddenly, someone tried to open the door and began banging on it when he found it was locked. Sarah had to suppress a gasp when she turned and saw it was Mayor Lewis. His face was red and blotchy, and his hair was missing in a few patches. He was sweating, putting off a strong, offensive body odor that Addie could pick up through the glass. *"He stinks,"* Addie informed Sarah.

"How?" Sarah asked, using her mind to speak so that Daisy could not hear their exchange.

"Something feral," Addie replied. *"Musky."*

Daisy cautiously cracked the door open. "Sorry, I'm closed. It's almost eight," she said apologetically. "Come back tomorrow, please."

"Daisy," he croaked, his voice hoarse. "I really need your help."

Daisy looked taken aback when she noticed how he looked. "What on earth? Are you sick?"

"Yes," he choked out roughly. "I feel terrible. Stomach cramps, my skin is driving me crazy—it's painfully itchy. Please, help me."

"Well . . . did you eat something bad?" Daisy was

carefully looking him over, clearly confused about what ailed him.

"No. I really don't know what's wrong. I think I'm allergic to stress, honestly," he replied.

Daisy opened the door the rest of the way and ushered him inside. He laid his arm on the counter and showed her the furious hives along the inside of it. "I've been under so . . . so much stress. Police interrogations and all of that. Someone framed me, and I am falling apart."

"Are you . . . are you sure you're not the victim of some dark magic?" Daisy asked, narrowing her eyes. "I've only seen something similar to this once before, on a woman who was targeted by a vindictive voodoo witch in Louisiana. The witch kept dunking a voodoo doll in boiling water so the victim was covered in burns."

Mayor Lewis looked uncomfortable. "I don't know who would target me, but at this point, I don't care. I just want relief."

"I can't help you if I don't know the source of the problem," Daisy said sympathetically. "I really need to know what you have touched, eaten, drank since the days before you fell ill. I also need to know if anyone might mean you harm."

"The whole town means me harm, it feels like!" he shouted belligerently.

Daisy shrank back from the force of his voice but then regained her composure. "I know how that feels," she said grimly. "In fact, I heard a rumor you might be behind some of the hatred that has been thrown my way."

"Why would I do that?" Mayor Lewis cried. Then he relented. "I didn't specifically say *your* name. I just mentioned, you know, the history of witches taking on wolf form in the woods and attacking people. I had to deflect attention away from me! I was framed!"

"Bring me a diary of your symptoms and your diet," was all Daisy replied.

"I have a craving for raw meat," Mayor Lewis admitted helplessly. "And these hives are from fleas."

Daisy's jaw fell open. "I'm sorry, what?" she asked, baffled.

"It just . . . started. I think it's some sort of infestation in my bed or something. But I need help." He made a cowering gesture that reminded Sarah of a scared dog. "I can't deal with this anymore."

"All right." Daisy backed away from him slowly, reluctant to turn her back to him to go through her bottles and bags on the shelves. But she soon located a tincture in a dark cobalt bottle. "I think you've been targeted by some sort of wolf spell. Bad shapeshifting magic, perhaps."

"Who would do that to me?" Mayor Lewis whined.

"I have no idea," Daisy told him, though Sarah had a feeling Daisy knew as well as she did that Madras might be behind all of this.

"Am I a werewolf now? I wasn't bitten by—by anything." He sounded terrified.

"There is no such thing as a werewolf. I think you were turned into a wolf and you are having trouble transitioning fully back into your human form. You really need to start acting more human, even if you feel the urge to act like a wolf. Stop eating raw meat—that's why your stomach is cramping. We humans can't digest that anymore, so don't let your cravings overpower your judgement. Take six drops of this in water twice a day and you should see an improvement. Oh, and here's this, for the fleas. Bathe with it twice a day and invest in a good insect repellent. Citronella on your neck can help." She produced a bag of natural flea powder for pets and a bottle of citronella from her shelf.

Mayor Lewis thanked her profusely as he paid for her products. As he scampered out of the apothecary, Sarah followed him out of the store, intrigued. But after he got home and drank a glass of water with Daisy's tincture in it, he relaxed on the couch, doing nothing criminal or even remotely suspicious.

Could he have been attacked by the same wolf that killed Mr. Atticos? Sarah wondered. *Or did Madras cast some sort of spell on him? If so, why did he claim he has no idea who did this to him? He could clear his name that way!* Then Sarah realized that the mayor probably had no idea that anyone in the police force would take him seriously. Even in a town named Witchland, there were many people who did not believe in or practice magic, and plenty more who thought witches were very real but also very evil. And with the current hysteria about wolves, undoubtedly he wanted to keep his ailment discreet!

Feeling bad for the mayor, Sarah decided to move on to find Levi. Sarah turned to ask Addie to sniff for him, then realized Addie was not with her.

When had Addie taken off? she wondered.

Sarah felt worried and decided to track down Addie first. She headed into the woods and soon found Addie, curled up in a little hole at the base of a tree with Kelvin. The two were snuggled together, murmuring loving nothings to each other.

Sarah smiled and chuckled. Hoping that one day she and Eli might do something similar, she returned to town to find Levi on her own.

It was not hard to locate Levi. He was leaving Geno's Ristorante Italiano with a box of pizza, just as they switched the sign on the door to 'Closed' behind him. It was now ten and quite dark, the stars and moon hidden by a thick blanket of clouds that threatened rain.

Levi walked by himself down a few streets. Sarah stayed several paces behind him, camouflaged and silent. The camouflage spell even kept her from making accidental noise because it made the elements around her comply, so even if she stepped on a twig, it would not snap.

Levi finally reached an abandoned house with a crumbling Victorian facade. Using a lighter from his pocket, he lit up the rickety steps and made his way inside. Sarah was stunned. How could someone stay in a dilapidated place like this? Why couldn't he get a hotel, like a normal person? This man looked guilty to the core!

She crept inside after him, trying to overcome her fear of empty, abandoned places. The inside of the house smelled like rotten wood. Parts of the ceiling had caved in over the hallway, and there were massive holes in the walls, exposing the beams and old lead pipes inside. Levi circumnavigated the boards and sheets of wood hanging from the ceiling and entered what was once a living room, which was in fairly good shape structurally. There, he sat on the bench of a derelict piano, where he tucked into his food.

Just then, his phone jingled. The blue light from the screen seemed out of place in the crumbling old house, which probably had not been occupied since the fifties. Sarah crept up behind him and looked over his shoulder so she could to see the texts.

"Where is my money?" The contact name displayed over the text was ML.

"I'm sending it now," Levi responded. "Do you have PayPal or Zelle?"

"Zelle," ML wrote back. Then he added, "Not under this number. This is a burner phone. Try this number." He typed a phone number with a Witchland area code.

Sarah felt her heart leap into her throat. Could ML be . . . Mayor Lewis? She had thought he was a nice person, but maybe there was more to his tragic werewolf story. Maybe he wasn't being framed, and all of the evidence pointed to him . . . because it was him!

Levi opened his Zelle app, entered the number, and sent ten thousand dollars. A message appeared that the money had been received. As Sarah strained to see the number and memorize it, she lost focus on her spell, and the floorboard under her foot creaked.

Levi jumped, toppling over the piano bench. Sarah immediately shifted back into her disguise, but Levi had already caught sight of her. "You witch!" he screamed. "I thought I felt watched!"

Sarah took off running. Boards lay in her way, but her camouflage spell allowed her to make her way through them unimpeded. Levi tripped behind her, landing on his knees. "Come back here!" he yelled pathetically as she got away.

Sarah heard him get on his phone and make a call. "Yeah, we have a serious problem!" he shouted. "It's that Spellwood witch! She took off and left!" Sarah realized that he could somehow still see her, even though she had camouflaged herself once again.

Knowing that she now had a target on her back, Sarah fled to the forest, where she knew she was at least safe. Coughing against the smoke, which was now thicker, Sarah found Addie and Kelvin. "Sorry to break this up, but I need you!" she yelled at Addie.

She caught Addie up on everything as they raced to the Leekins' fence. *"How did he still see you when you went back into your disguise?"* Addie mused.

"I have no idea," Sarah said, also perplexed. "It's like . . . maybe he has access to some sort of magic?"

"You think he knows magic?" Addie inquired. *"He didn't strike me as the type."*

"Nor did I think so, but nothing is as it seems, I guess. I even thought Mayor Lewis was a nice guy, but I have to find out for sure now." Sarah shook her head.

"I always hated him," Addie growled.

"How could he have fooled me? I am supposed to have great intuition," Sarah went on. "Even you knew."

"I didn't know anything but that he gives off bad vibes," Addie replied. *"You're human, you try to see the best in everything. I'm a canine, I just see things as they are."*

They found a Leekin sitting on a fallen tree trunk near the Leekin fence, whittling a twig into some sort of tool. He set his whittling down when he saw them approach and rolled his eyes. "It's late, and I want to relax," he groaned.

"I am in serious trouble, and you guys are supposed to help me," Sarah told him. "Where's Clover Figcreek?"

"They're busy trying to fight the fire," the Leekin replied grumpily. "Left me here to assist you if you needed it, and I guess you need it." He sighed as he stood and dusted off his legs. "Can it at least wait until morning?"

"Sure, but I need it done first thing. I can't be seen in town because I think I just made a powerful enemy. He'll be looking for me. I need you to infiltrate Mayor Lewis's bank account and find out if he received ten thousand dollars," Sarah instructed.

The Leekin sighed again. "And I thought I could sleep in tomorrow."

"Do you want me to push you off that log you're balancing on?" Addie threatened.

The Leekin backed away from her, looking scared.

"Well, no," he snapped, turning slightly blue. "I would get hurt!"

"Then do it. It's for the good of the town," Sarah told him.

He sighed wearily and alighted on his little brown wings. "You got it. Now I'm off to bed."

Sarah then returned to the apothecary, where she knew she might be safer than Michael's house.

***

Sarah found Daisy asleep. She woke her and hastily recounted the entire night while huddling in the doorway, hoping no one saw her. She wanted to use her camouflage, but she needed Daisy to be able to see her.

"Put your camouflage on. I can see through it with a simple spell," Daisy told her calmly. "Now come in and start from the beginning."

Once inside, Sarah related the events of the night more clearly. Daisy nodded slowly along to the story, only interrupting once: "I could tell someone was there, watching me. I thought about doing a vision blocking spell on you so you couldn't spy on me, but then I figured, let whoever it is watch! I didn't get an evil feeling from you, which is why I wasn't too concerned, but I didn't know who you were."

"Sorry. I felt bad about spying, but I was actually

trying to exonerate you. And instead I ended up getting dirt on Mayor Lewis!" Sarah told her.

"I had a weird feeling when the mayor said he was a werewolf." Daisy shook her head. "See, werewolves don't really exist."

"They don't?" Sarah, though exhausted, was sitting up with Daisy in the little back room where she kept her cot and stove. Addie was curled up at her toes, dreaming of Kelvin, judging by the happy way she kept sighing and curling up tighter. "I thought were-wolves were like a quintessential part of magic," Sarah added.

"There is no such thing," Daisy replied softly. "Shapeshifting into any animal is a thing, yes. But you cannot infect someone to shapeshift automatically into a wolf every full moon. I'm sure there's a dark spell to accomplish that if you really want to, but . . . it really isn't done. And it could easily be reversed if someone did try it."

"Is it possible Madras put such a spell on Mayor Lewis?" Sarah asked. "He doesn't strike me as a bad man. . . ."

"No, but he's a weak man." Daisy stood up. "He has always avoided me and mistreated me in town hall meetings. If he sees me at the grocer's or anywhere else around town, he doesn't even say hi. Yet when he needs me, he sure comes knocking."

"Maybe his attitude about magic will change now," Sarah suggested. "Maybe he's a victim of Madras's."

"More like a victim of greed." Daisy shook her head. "He is a man who can be bought. He was almost bought by those greedy developers who wanted to mow down the forest; though he drug his feet on the deal because he likes the natural landscape here, he didn't say no to the money. That's why I'm glad you have that Leekin looking into his account. And to answer your question, I don't know what is wrong with him specifically, but I don't feel he's the innocent victim of some dark magic. I think he has some hand in all of this."

"I was really hoping not, but we will see what the Leekin finds tomorrow." Sarah sighed. "Now I need my sleep."

"So do I!" Daisy said.

Sarah awoke at dawn to a whisper in her ear. She rolled onto her side and saw the Leekin standing there, looking even more irritable than the night before.

"The money is in there," he told her gruffly.

Sarah bolted up on her makeshift bed. The fire had died, and there was a distinct chill in the room that made her wince. "What? The ten thousand is in there?"

"Yes. He received it last night around ten twenty-five p.m. Anything else?" The Leekin crossed his arms, tapping his fingers on his elbows with impatience.

"No, thank you very much, though." Sarah gathered her red curly hair back into a ponytail and started to brace herself for getting up into the cold air.

Daisy heard her stirring and rolled over in her cot to survey her. "The money was in there?" she asked.

Sarah nodded grimly. "I guess I know who ML is. Now I want to know why he's in cahoots with Levi and why he's showing signs of being part wolf. Pretty odd there were wolf hairs on Mr. Atticos's body, don't you agree?"

Daisy sat up. "See if Jenna will give you a hair from evidence. I can probably look at it and see if there is some residual magic on it, maybe a shapeshifting spell."

"Sure thing." Sarah tugged on her coat and zipped it up. "I hope she's awake this early."

"She's a cop. And crime never sleeps, so neither does she," Daisy told her. Then she smirked. "And I guess neither do we."

Sarah found Jenna at home. Jenna reluctantly agreed to give her a few hairs. "I could lose my job over this, so you better keep it hush-hush," she reminded Sarah as she led her to the police station's evidence room and unlocked the thick steel door. "How many hairs does she need? I can't give you the whole sample."

"She said just a few," Sarah replied. "Man, I need coffee."

"You'd make a great cop," Jenna joked as she returned with a few hairs in a fresh evidence bag. "Don't worry about returning those. There are plenty in the evidence file, and some have already been sent to the forensics lab for DNA analysis. That's how they know it's genuine wolf fur."

"Thanks so much," Sarah told her, placing the hair sample in her coat pocket. "By the way, I was wondering if I could try something in your office? I need your computer—do you have a music app?"

"Sure," Jenna said, looking at her quizzically. "What for?"

"I want to try something." Sarah followed Jenna into her office, where she laid Lativia's spellbook on the desk. She had been carrying it with her in her handbag since the day before, when she had been experimenting with it. Its heft felt like a bowling ball in her bag.

Sarah began to search for colonial music from the late 1600s on Jenna's desktop. Jenna leaned against the door, watching and smiling as she realized what Sarah was doing. As the music began to play, Sarah opened the book, and cried out in joy when she saw written words start to sprawl across the pages in time to the song's beat.

"I got it!" she shouted. "I just had to find music from Lativia's time when she wrote this."

"Genius," Jenna agreed. Jenna moved to stand next to Sarah and look at the spells, entranced by what she was seeing. She, too, had wanted to see the spells that she had long played a part in protecting and upholding. Here was the town's history, as well as the energetic fabric that had sheltered it from the evil that had occurred within it lately. It was a beautiful sight to behold, like artwork in a newly unveiled museum exhibit. It didn't hurt that Lativia had extraordinary penmanship.

Sarah began to hastily jot down spells that had to do with blocking fire and calming agitated or aggressive people while she waited for the music to upload to her phone. She knew those would be the handiest at this time. "I wish I knew how to just memorize these spells, but the language is so old that it's lost on me," she told Jenna.

Jenna nodded. "I think the heart you put into the spell matters a bit more than the actual syntax," she said. "Lativia's spells have been handed down orally, and they still work, even though the words change.

Magic is about heart, energy, the soul. What you put into it is what you get out of it."

Sarah found this simple explanation of magic so much clearer than anything she had heard before. It made perfect sense to her. As she scanned for more spells that could be useful in a confrontation with Madras, she found a few very long, complex ones that were too much to write down. She decided to commit them to memory, as Jenna had suggested, by focusing on the meaning behind them instead of the precise wording. She found that they were remarkable for building up her courage.

"Thanks so much!" Sarah shouted when she had what she needed. She gave Jenna a quick, grateful hug before hurrying back to Daisy's, leaving the spellbook on Jenna's desk, unwilling to carry its hefty bulk up the mountain.

Sarah handed Daisy the few hairs in the evidence bag. "It's all Jenna could give me without raising suspicion," she apologized.

"Perfectly fine, it's just enough." Daisy laid the hairs on a dish and began to prod at them with a strange silver rod. As she began to hum to clear her mind, Sarah went to Javacadabra. Usually she only drank tea, but today called for some serious coffee.

Karen, Susie's wife and business partner, was working today. She was giving Susie time to stay home with their little visitor, Claire. As she gushed about how much Claire had grown in both magic and maturity, while pulling out a double espresso shot for Sarah's coffee, Sarah heard a commotion outside. She peered out the window and saw a massive mob of people gathering in front of the apothecary's courtyard gate and the coffee shop, shouting, "Kill the witch! Kill the witch!" A woman with a baby held to her chest in a Moby wrap bore a banner that read, 'Kill our people no more! Stop the evil!' Another man, whom Sarah vaguely recognized as a pastor from a local church, was climbing onto a makeshift pulpit of milk crates, from where he started hoarsely shouting Scripture at the top of his lungs. Apparently, the anti-witch sentiment that Mayor Lewis had planted had been growing into something very large and ugly.

"Oh, no," Sarah said to Addie. "Poor Daisy."

Karen gulped and shook her head. "This is bad for business. I'm locking my doors." She raised a hand of apology to the other patron in the shop and added, "Sorry, Charlie, but you might want to go home now."

"Oh, no, I'm staying right where I am," the old man she was referring to said. "I won't go out there in this riot for anything."

"Try that calming spell of Lativia's. You knew you might need it for moments like these," Addie reminded Sarah.

Sarah hastily put a camouflage over them both. Charlie stared as they both disappeared, now blending in perfectly with the background of tiles, chairs, and the glass case full of baked goods around them. Then he shook his head, understanding that such things happened in Witchland, and returned to reading his newspaper.

Sarah and Addie hurried outside, where they were near enough to the mob to be effective with the calming spell. Sarah was not sure if she would be as powerful from a distance, at least not at this point in her training. Physical limitations like distance and time and even steel doors did not stop most witches, but it took a lot of dedication and concentration to overcome such things.

With a shaky hand, Sarah pulled the sheets of paper upon which she had scribbled some of Lativia's spells from her pocket and located the one for a calming spell. As she began to recite the words, filling in some of the more archaic ones with her own, she glanced up to see if there were any results.

Sadly, the mob continued to yell, clearly unable to give up their witch hunt.

"Why isn't this working?" Sarah cried out in despair. "Am I doing it wrong? Am I just not powerful enough?" Her newfound belief in her own magic rapidly began to wane.

"*Uh, Sarah? Look,*" Addie answered. She was pointing her nose toward Mount Katribus and the forest.

Since the fire had started, a slight drift of smoke had swept down from the mountain, adding the scent of tragedy to Witchland's atmosphere. But the fog now wafting down was much thicker, and it did not carry any odor. Sarah stared, transfixed, as the ominous gray vapor began to curl around tree leaves, stone walls, and corners, flooding every inch of the quaint forest town. It had an oily effect, coating everything in its path with darkness as it moved on to envelope more of the town. Drops of it dripped from the trees, sliding along the ground.

"What the heck is that?" she whispered, fear tightening her throat.

"*Some kind of spiritual miasma,*" Addie mused. *"Notice how no one seems to notice it but us?"*

The crowd was still protesting Daisy's shop, apparently impervious to the strange fog that was now obfuscating Sarah's vision. It felt like nothing but normal air on her skin, even though she could see it coating her arms and rolling down to drip off of her fingertips with the consistency of a half gas, half vapor. She blinked, but her vision was now dimmed.

Sarah got a bad feeling that this fog had something to do with Madras. It was coming from the mountain, where the fire raged and where Kelvin had spotted the demonic wolf. Perhaps it was intended to block her magic, or at least agitate people. Either way, it was clearly a problem. It would make sense that Madras would do this to lower any defenses the town's witches may level against her and to create chaos.

Skin prickling, Sarah and Addie rushed back into the apothecary. There they found Daisy, also camouflaging herself and hastily putting on layers to go outside.

"Do you see that fog?" Sarah demanded.

"Yes. I've never seen anything like it, but it is very bad," Daisy replied. "Some dark magic, for sure."

"Come with me to the mountain!" Sarah cried. "We have to get you out of here."

Daisy just nodded numbly. "I was one step ahead of you, dear." She fixed her purple-rimmed glasses, adjusted her dreadlocks under her hat, pulled on her patchwork quilt coat, and began to jog alongside Sarah. Despite being in her fifties, she was just as nimble and fit as Sarah was. Sarah briefly admired her health. *Must be all of those herbal potions and tinctures she takes,* Sarah mused, making a mental note to try Daisy's routine for herself to halt aging.

The three commenced their climb toward Mount Katribus. Their breathing soon became labored as they toiled up the steep path in the bad air. The fog was especially thick in the woods, still rolling down through the trees to blanket the town, and it was now mixed with heavy smoke. Sarah coughed into the crook of her elbow as her eyes stung and watered; Addie had to stop several times to gag.

"I think the fog's whole purpose is both to obscure everyone's reason and incite violence," Daisy mused. "I am trying to think of an equivalent to it, but I can't. I never studied dark magic, and that is all that this is."

"It definitely blocked my magic," Sarah explained. "I tried to calm the mob with one of Lativia's spells, and obviously with no luck."

"*This is horrible! What can we do with your magic blocked?*" Addie whined, fear lacing her voice. "*I really hope Kelvin hasn't been hurt.*" She glanced at the woods, as if searching for him in the smoky trees.

"I hope he is, too, girl. Madras seems to be more powerful than my magic or Lativia's," Sarah agreed anxiously. Her stomach began to hurt, as worry frantically gnawed at it. "What if I can't vanquish her?"

"Remember your coven," Daisy replied. "You are not alone! When Lativia was too weak to save herself, her sisters helped her. We all have weaknesses and feeble moments. That's why we band together."

Sarah nodded, feeling a bit reassured. "I was wondering if I could use Madras's history as her weakness? After all, she was burned at the stake, and now she's using fire and heat and smoke. It must be connected."

"Sometimes, to defeat the enemy, you have to think

like the enemy," Daisy agreed as she struggled to catch her breath. "Madras is an angry woman—or, I should say, spirit. She only wants one thing, and that's revenge. In revenge, she can get power. But her thirst for revenge also makes her weak, impulsive, prone to mistakes."

"She feels powerless at heart," Sarah realized. "Or otherwise she wouldn't want revenge that badly."

"Bingo." Daisy grinned. "Nothing like a lawyer to find and exploit someone's weaknesses."

"Hey," Sarah protested with a laugh. She was used to lawyer jokes. It felt good to have Daisy's company in this moment, but she desperately wished more witches could join them. She would even take Harriet's annoying presence now! She regretted not taking more time to fetch Margaret, Hua, and Jenna, but she and Daisy had been in too much of a hurry to escape the impending riot in the village and face the evil fog brewing in the forest.

Toward the top of the peak, they fell into a heavy silence as they steeled themselves for what lay ahead. The silence lay between them like a blanket. Every few moments, they had to stop and recover from the bad air. Their lungs were burning, and their breath screamed in their sore throats.

They finally reached the top, after what felt like forever. Sarah realized how much her jaw hurt from clenching it in nervousness—her stomach also still ached. She despised the cloying, greasy feeling of the miasma that had bathed her skin.

Here, the fog and the smoke made visibility extremely limited. Up ahead, flames looked like evil spirits, performing an ugly dance in a ring around the clearing where the ghosts congregated. Sarah could see malicious faces forming and then disappearing in the fierce yellow and orange. She imagined surrounding herself, Addie, and Daisy in cool mist, which deflected the angry heat of the fire so that they could step through into the clearing. Daisy helped her, and the heat dissipated.

Standing in the center of the ghostly clearing was the ghost of a woman who looked exactly like Lativia but much thinner and paler. The red of her hair had turned rusty, unlike the rich red of Lativia's, and it hung lank and greasy down to her knees. Sores covered her skin, which Sarah soon realized were burns from the fire that had killed her. She stood beside the spirit of Lativia, whose ghostly glow was dimmer than before. Lativia was completely bound to a ghostly blue stake by ghostly blue shackles. Blue blood dripped from wounds on her face, staining her white gown. No other ghosts were visible in the clearing.

"Sarah, you finally came," Lativia uttered faintly. "She finally defeated me and put me in these shackles."

Lativia struggled against her bindings but was not able to move much. It was clear by the wreckage of the clearing and the blast marks in the ground that the two witches had been dueling for quite some time, with very powerful magic.

"I'm here to rescue you, don't you worry," Sarah shouted. *Is it even possible to rescue someone who is already dead?*

When Madras turned to view her new visitors, her eyes blazed with hatred. She had deep grooves in the skin around her mouth, the deepest frown lines Sarah had ever seen. Her nails were extremely long and caked with filth, and she raised a bony finger to point at Sarah.

"My great-great-grandniece," she said. Her voice stunned Sarah; it was beautiful and mellifluous, not at all the cruel, shrill cackle Sarah had expected. "I have been looking forward to finally meeting you."

"Why do you have Lativia restrained like that?" Sarah demanded. "You need to let her go. She's your own sister!"

Madras sighed and stepped closer toward Sarah. Daisy's breath caught in her throat in a terrified gasp to be so near such astonishing evil. Addie raised her hackles and began to growl threateningly as she backed away into Sarah's legs. Sarah tried to back away as well, but felt the heat of the flames on her back and instead stood her ground, trying hard not to betray her inner horror. The energy coming off of Madras was intense, overpowering; she also smelled putrid, like sulfur, chemical fire, and rotten meat.

"I'm afraid you have been misled with a common family myth. Lativia has lied to you, and I'm here to explain the truth," Madras said, her voice heavy with sadness.

"Lativia would never lie to me," Sarah responded with a curt laugh. "Why would I ever believe someone like you over her?"

"Because she has stolen everything from me and framed me for her crimes! You have been raised to think she is the heroine, when in fact she is the villain. Please just listen; after all, you are my family, too." Madras bowed her head slightly, her lank hair falling in front of her face.

"For centuries, I have lived with the injustice of my sister's lies. I have been blocked out of my rightful home, my rightful legacy, and my honor. And I have been banished to roam the woods, feared and hated, all over a misunderstanding. You see, your beloved Lativia is not as innocent as she claims. There is a reason she survived the witch trials and I didn't; she betrayed me." Madras turned and pointed at Lativia. "She was the one who fed me to the witch hunters, who told them what I was doing, and she didn't think they would come after her, too! She called on the coven to help her and to abandon me by telling them I was doing dark magic. I was never doing anything evil, just unconventional, and she couldn't stand that I was becoming a stronger witch than she was!"

"Sorcery and borrowing the power of demons does not make you a powerful witch! Only an empty vessel for evil to take hold of," Lativia cried. "Sorcery ruined you, Madras."

Madras snorted. "You can't simply dismiss sorcery if you have never tried it. You are speaking from ignorance and that witchy elitism you all have." She exhaled and turned to Sarah and Daisy again. "Have either of you ever tried to summon a spirit?"

"Never," Daisy said firmly.

"No." Sarah shook her head. She had no idea how to go about that, but it sounded bad. Lativia's spellbook had mentioned nothing about summoning spirits—that she had seen—which was probably a sign it was not a type of magic she needed to meddle with.

"That's because you two have been taught by Lativia, and she has left out some important details. I could teach you so much you don't know, both of you— but especially you, Sarah. You will go from novice witch to the most powerful witch in the world in days!" Her eyes glittered as she surveyed her descendent. "I know how you feel insecure and worried about your powers. You have repressed them for a long time; they are quite weak. But I could resurrect them and make them ten times as powerful!"

"Stop! I wouldn't want to learn anything from you," Sarah responded. It unnerved her that Madras had caught onto her greatest insecurity at the moment, the same strategy she had prepared herself. "Just look at you now, compared to Lativia. It is clear something has been eating at you; your spirit looks sick!"

"*And smells worse,*" Addie added.

Madras recoiled in rage, clearly incensed by both comments. "Well, I'm sorry I haven't had Leekins pampering me on a throne for centuries! Life has been hard after death! I'm not petty enough to worry about whether or not my sister is prettier than me. That's for the lowly men to squabble over."

"You have always resented my looks, since the day Richard Hornby kissed me instead of you at the schoolhouse," Lativia piped up.

"Be quiet, you!" Madras snarled. "Maybe you won some silly boy when we were girls, but look at who's in chains now! I would have to say I won," she gloated. "Now you can face the same fate I did while I take back what's rightfully mine."

"You can't burn her at the stake," Sarah argued. "She's already long dead!"

Madras laughed and tilted her head to the side as

she surveyed Lativia. "She may be dead, but she can still feel. She can feel what I did as the flames consumed me. She can scream as she watches me take over her precious little town."

"I can't let you do this," Sarah said, shaking her head. "I'm the protector of the forest and of Witchland by extension. You may not take my home over, not on my watch."

Madras turned back to face Sarah as she said, "You are still ridiculously deluded. It's understandable—Lativia gets to people like that. She's been doing it for centuries. That's why she's been heralded as the greatest light witch of all time." She laughed bitterly. "Makes me sick! When you realize that I speak the truth, you might just reconsider. You could be the first witch to know the truth and fight for what is actually right, as opposed to all of these silly, deluded witches you've been training under." Madras made a disparaging face and gesture toward Daisy.

"If Lativia is evil and you are good, then why did you allow bad things to happen in Witchland? You've been stirring up violence, and you killed the poor town clerk!" Sarah countered.

Madras sighed. "You don't understand; sometimes casualties are necessary to win a war. I didn't kill anyone, but I had to allow things to happen as they were meant to. I simply put the motions in place for the town to sort out its own problems and allow me to step in and kick its worst cancer out—Lativia!"

"But that man died because of you!" Sarah felt tears burning in her eyes, not just from the smoke but from the grief of all that Madras had done. She could not believe that Madras could stand there, defending her actions as if they were right. It appeared that Madras genuinely believed that she had been wronged and she had a right to Witchland.

"There is more to life than just being alive; you can enjoy much more power and freedom when you are no longer anchored to a body. Mr. Atticos is simply released into the spirit world—his historical research is much easier for him now," Madras replied coolly.

"That's not your right to take his life like that, though," Addie spoke up.

Madras's lips curled back, and she started to say something rude to Addie, but bit her tongue. Glancing briefly at Sarah, it was clear she realized that being mean to the dog would only make Sarah dislike her more. "You are one cute dog, and an even better wolf," she decided to say instead. "I am a wolf spirit myself. See, we all have a lot more in common than we think."

"You are a demon wolf, not even a real wolf," Sarah shot back. "And I know you killed Mr. Atticos because he was killed by a demonized shapeshifter."

Daisy started to say something, but Madras cut her

off. "You may be a good lawyer, and you may have the makings to be a good witch one day, but you are not such a good sleuth. Again, I could help you with that. I could teach you everything you need to know to be good at everything you try in life! That's your ultimate goal, is it not, to do your best?"

Sarah felt sickened that Madras knew her so well.

"I understand you, Sarah, because I am just like you. If you simply opened your eyes, you would realize that we would make a great team, you and I. Your powers combined with mine? We could rule this town and, eventually, the whole world!" Madras stretched her arms over her head, her face lit by the flames around the clearing as well as her own internal cruel light.

"Don't do it," Addie cautioned.

"I would never do it," Sarah replied to Addie resolutely. Then she turned to Madras and began to shout a freezing spell she had learned to stop Madras.

> *With this air as cold as ice,*
> *Be concise!*
> *Be precise!*
> *Once, twice, thrice!*

Madras simply laughed and held up her hand. A blue lightning bolt left her palm and collided in the air with Sarah's invisible magic. "If you want to do this the hard way, we can," she told Sarah breezily. "Just think, if I can have your precious Lativia like this"—she gestured toward Lativia bound to the stake—"then imagine what I can do to you! You're just a novice, a weakling human, and I'm an infinite spirit."

"She's just trying to get to your head! She can't physically do anything to you, so she has to use mental manipulation!" Daisy shouted. "Don't fear her!"

"I'm more than just a novice," Sarah snarled. "I'm a Spellwood!"

Madras pretended not to hear Sarah as she whirled on Daisy with fury. "Oh, I can certainly physically hurt her. I can do anything I want. Just you watch." To prove her point, she promptly hit Daisy with a spell that toppled her over on the ground. Daisy moaned in pain. "That was a spiritual punch to the face!" Madras giggled maniacally.

Then, with a snap of her fingers, a human came crashing through the flames, hurtling toward Sarah.

It was Levi! Sarah gasped as she recognized his face, contorted with rage.

Levi barreled at her like a quarterback. She let out an involuntary scream as he scooped her up effortlessly under his arm, aided by the element of surprise and his inhuman strength.

"I think you two have already met," Madras said.

"Levi here is actually one of my most loyal followers. I call my followers *truth speakers,* because they don't believe Lativia's lies."

Levi scooped up Daisy under his other arm and dragged both witches to a spot next to Lativia. It was only then that Sarah noticed two makeshift wooden stakes and thick sisal rope lying on the ground there.

"My truth speakers are richly rewarded for their loyalty. Levi here? I've given him incredible power, including Herculean strength," Madras drawled on. "He's just an example of what I could do for you, Sarah. Since you're family, I would actually do so much more for you than for him. I would make you the most powerful witch in the whole world, a true Spell-wood! You would no longer be limited and blinded by Lativia!"

Lativia began to sob in desperation as Levi raised the stakes with one arm and restrained both women with the other. In one deft movement, he managed to lash both women to the stakes. Sarah attempted to fight him off, but he kept overpowering her, pinning her body against the stake and immobilizing her. *How can he be this strong with just two arms? Madras really has given him some power. I wonder if it's the demons inside of her, giving her all of this magical ability.*

Daisy did not try to fight at all, and Sarah prayed that perhaps Daisy had some other trick tucked up her sleeve. Daisy did seem awfully quiet, which was unusual for her spunky personality.

Finished with his task, Levi backed up and surveyed them, leering proudly. Madras nodded at him approvingly. "See, isn't revenge sweet?" she purred, petting his shoulder, her hand passing through his flesh.

Levi nodded, a sadistic grin spreading across his face. "John would be proud," he said. "I heard how he and his business partner tied you up, Sarah. Bringing back sweet memories?"

I failed, Sarah thought miserably as she tugged at the ropes binding her arms and found them to be totally secure. *Who is going to save me now?* She eyed Addie, who cowered by the flames, looking crushed that she could not save her person yet again.

Sarah felt a sinking feeling in her stomach and a bristling on her skin. Since she felt truly scared, her skin was turning to wood—but being wood was not going to help her here! She remembered her Spellwood propensity for burning easily. *If no one is going to save me right now, then I have to save myself,* she realized.

"I wish I had learned a spell for this. I didn't realize I would be in this situation. Do you know of any spells?" she murmured out of the corner of her mouth to Daisy.

Daisy simply shook her head. Her lips were

pressed into a flat line, and Sarah realized she was shaking from her feet to her head.

Daisy was scared, too.

Sarah began to sense her hair curling up and turning into leaves, while her skin was now totally covered in scaly bark. *I have to get out of these ropes soon or I'll turn into a crisp! Think, Sarah, think!* she thought desperately.

"Ah, my little wooden doll." Madras laughed, tracing the curve of Sarah's chin with her nail. Sarah's body had become completely wooden. Cold jolted through Sarah where Madras had touched her. "This doesn't have to be how it ends, you know. You don't have to meet the same fate as your ancestor. Just let go, let me take care of you, and all will be well."

"I would rather die," Sarah spat back. She realized, as she said it, that she meant every word. Dying this way was not her intention, but it would surely beat being a dark witch—hurting people and betraying those who trusted her most—to protect the forest and the town. "See, you think you know me so well, but you got a few things wrong. I don't want power, or revenge. Yes, I want to be the best witch I can be, but you have underestimated one of my strongest qualities: I will do everything the *right* way. That's how I endured bullying in school even though I was a Spellwood and I could have magically sealed their mouths shut, that's how I got through law school when I wanted to give up or cheat on an exam, and that's how I survived my divorce and losing my job when I could have just curled into a little ball and cried."

Madras surveyed her, clearly not liking what she had to say. It was clear she was trying to come up with a new angle. Then she thought of one and gestured toward Levi. "Don't act so hoity-toity. You want to be great; we all do. That kind of physical strength Levi has and so much more could be yours, my dear. Did Lativia give you anything great like that? No, probably just some cryptic message about finding things out for yourself, huh? And a spellbook full of fluff." Madras laughed heartily. "Calming spells and blending in with trees! Please! Why bother with that stuff when you can seize whatever you want and control minds? You can rule the world quite easily with *real* magic."

Wolves! Sarah suddenly remembered. "Addie!" she screamed.

"I'm trying!" Addie cried. *"But she's blocking me. I can't transform."* Addie looked terrified as she struggled to save Sarah. Watching not just one but two of her persons die would be heart-wrenching to the poor dog.

I can't let this happen. I can't die. I have so much to live for, and so many people who depend on me, Sarah resolved once and for all. *I have Addie to live for, and*

Witchland, and the Leekins, and this forest. I have to preserve Lativia's legacy and fight evil, as that's my purpose. And I want to kiss Eli! Finally!

With her new resolve, she felt a flush of something strange, something she had never felt before, which started in her heart and then rapidly began to spread throughout her body.

First, she felt her skin itch. The bark covering her skin was being replaced by thick, silver fur! Then, with a slight pain, her nails began to recede into their beds, and claws erupted out in their place. With fascination, Sarah watched her legs shorten and felt her neck and head change shape and her nose grow into a snout. The ropes suddenly fell limp around her. Her muscles bulged and became sinewy and tough. Her jaw hurt briefly as her mouth filled with large teeth and canines.

Without the restraints holding her up to the stake, she hit the ground on all fours. Her paws spread wide on the ground, and she was mesmerized by her strange new sense of balance, so different from the way she usually experienced it.

Am I a wolf? she wondered briefly. When she looked down, she realized that she resembled Addie, sleek and strong. The sleek silvery fur coating her body fascinated her.

Levi shrieked with terror when he saw her powerful, lanky new form. He ran toward her to restrain her, but she evaded him, running into the ring of fire surrounding the clearing. Levi attempted to chase her, but when he came too close to the fire, he cried out and retreated, nursing the burns on his hand. Sarah was protected from the flames because she had caught Madras off guard and was now able to practice magic again without being blocked. The miasma around her had even dissipated momentarily, no longer being generated by Madras in all of her shock and outrage.

Madras began to recite a spell in an unidentifiable tongue. Her face had acquired a deathly green pallor as she mustered all of her evil powers to vanquish Sarah. "Another nasty little wolf witch, huh? I got just the antidote for you!" she screeched.

Sarah found herself unable to move, held spellbound by Madras's intense gaze.

"Don't look at her!" Daisy screamed.

But Sarah was now completely paralyzed. She could not look away now. Her brief moment of valor as a wolf was still no match for Madras.

Just then, there was a flash of light, and someone hurtled through the flames. Sarah felt overwhelmed with joy when she recognized the cop uniform and long brown hair of Jenna.

CHAPTER NINE

In a courageous yell, Jenna pointed at Addie and uttered a command, "Turn into a wolf!"

Addie, who had been struggling to transform into her power spirit against Madras's insidious blocking magic, was now able to suddenly burst into her wolf form. Sarah then remembered reading that Addie, as a power spirit, was required to obey the commands of gatekeepers and their assistants—that law of magic was far more powerful than the one created by Madras's blocking spell.

With a fierce snarl, Addie lunged toward Daisy to tear off her restraints. Levi cowered from her in fear, unwilling to fight her off despite Madras's urging.

"No!" Madras cried out, dismay apparent in her voice. She was not expecting a paranormal gatekeeper to come to the rescue, wielding Lativia's spellbook and all of its magic. She realized that perhaps there was a match for Madras's acquired demonic powers, after all.

Addie tore through Lativia's ghostly restraints with her teeth. Then she turned to Daisy. The two witches ran off to the other side of the flames and lowered themselves to the ground, trying to regain their strength and their bearings. Madras attempted to chase them, but was distracted by Sarah, who began to shout to Jenna.

"We have to undo the blocking magic and bring forth the Leekins! I know they're up here, fighting the fire, but Madras must have done something to immobilize them or they would be here fighting alongside us!" Sarah shouted to Jenna. Her wolf form had rapidly receded back into human form as soon as she was distracted by Jenna's presence, but her voice still came out oddly canine, more of a raspy bark than her usual sweet, mellifluous vocals. Jenna stared at her with a bit of shock before nodding vigorously.

Jenna struggled to open a music app on her phone after digging it out from deep within her pocket. Turning it to top volume, she held it near the book to illuminate the writing and then began to flip desperately through the pages, trying to locate the correct spell.

"Seriously? That is just plain silly. You think your

little book will defeat me?" Madras declared haughtily. "Lativia has never been any match for me!"

"Learning from others instead of dismissing and belittling them is the true sign of strength and wisdom," Daisy spoke up, courage making her voice firm. "Maybe you are a great witch, but that does not make your sister weak. You should have worked with her instead of against her. Together, the two of you could have made such a wonderful difference in the world."

"Why would I work with my sister?" Madras snapped. "She's the one who always belittled me. Made me less than."

"I never meant to do that," Lativia spoke up. She was now standing and had crossed the threshold of fire once again to confront her sister. Her ghostly frame vibrated with strength, not fear. Sarah had the sense that something very powerful was about to happen; the very atmosphere buzzed with magic.

"You always did," Madras said coarsely. "You enjoyed being the center of attention, having everyone fawn over you while making me look bad. You still do it now, and we've been dead for centuries!"

"That's not true! I just try to do what's right and to help you find your way back to the light!" Lativia cried. She then raised her ghostly hands with a roar of rage and sent forth a burst of golden magic. Though Sarah did not know the specific spell Lativia used, she sensed it was a cleansing spell, meant to vanquish evil and purify her sister's spirit.

The instant the spell hit Madras, she paled and reeled back. Her form began to split into several entities, all hideous faces that snarled and spoke in different tongues. Faces of monsters, demons, and ghouls. The image of Madras completely disappeared, revealing that it had only been an illusion.

"Look at you now!" Lativia sobbed. "You're not even yourself. You've been taken over by these other spirits, totally possessed. You were my sister!" The pain of the betrayal was clear in her voice, an old wound that had never truly healed.

"And I am ten times as powerful as you because of our collective strength! We are Madras times ten, and we're here to take back what's ours!" the different spirits managed to say at once, their multiple hissing voices dissonant and jarring. Then they merged back together with a sucking sound, taking the form of Madras once again.

Madras hurled herself at Lativia, wrapping her ghostly hands around Lativia's ghostly throat. The two grappled and fell to the ground in a headlock. Their faces strained with the effort of their spiritual entanglement; it was clear that they were an equal match.

Addie let out a bloodcurdling snarl and lunged at

the pair. As she struggled to guard Lativia's throat, another wolf form burst through the trees. Sarah struggled to see who it was. At first, she thought it might be Michael. But she was stunned when she realized it was, in fact, Kelvin—Addie's sweetheart.

"I'm not going to let you die!" he yelled ferociously. He hurled himself into the fray.

Addie briefly looked at him, and the fear in her eyes was instantly replaced with love and gratitude. Then she returned to her task at hand, and the two wolves managed to come between Madras and Lativia. Madras stood up and backed away from their gnashing teeth, knowing that they could hurt her even in her spiritual state since they were animals. For a moment, she let her guard down, and the fog began to lift.

Just then, Sarah and Jenna finally located a spell that explained how to totally lift the miasmic fog blocking everyone's magic. Sarah took advantage of Madras's lapse in concentration to utter it. She regained her wolf form and half shouted, half growled a spell at the top of her lungs. The air suddenly cleared, and Sarah sucked in fresh air with great relief. Instantly, several ghosts and Leekins appeared. Clover Figcreek fluttered near Sarah's face, frantically shouting about how Sarah needed to put out the fire.

Next, Sarah shouted another spell to put out the magical flames. The flames danced back, turned green, and then flickered out of existence, leaving behind only a few tendrils of acrid smoke as evidence they had ever been there. Sarah noticed only a small amount of damage had been done to the surrounding forest; the trees looked like they would survive, even though their sides facing the clearing were scorched.

"I don't think so!" Madras screamed in rage. A fireball exploded from her fingertips and rippled over the forest, engulfing the trees and wildlife in fire and smoke. The heat of the fireball singed Sarah's wolf fur as it seared past her. She realized that she felt heat much more in her wolf body, cloaked as it was in heavy fur and protective fat.

"Eli!" Jenna shrieked. Sarah noticed that Jenna no longer had any eyebrows or eyelashes and her cheeks were extremely red with light burns. "Eli is in the woods! We have to help him!" She frantically turned to leave the clearing, but was halted by the impenetrable wall of fire she encountered, which was much worse than before. "I can protect myself from the flames, but Eli can't," she sobbed in despair.

"Help us conjure rain!" Clover Figcreek shouted to Sarah. "The fire is spreading now!"

Sarah realized that she wasn't getting anywhere with the spellbook now. Thankfully, the book had been preserved from the flames, probably by some protective spell of Lativia's, but Jenna's phone had melted from the heat of the fireball, so it was no longer playing the colonial music necessary to unlock the writing. Hurling the hefty book in her wolf-mouth to the ground, Sarah shut her eyes and began to focus on rain. The smell of it, the sweet wetness bathing the forest, the salvation from heat and fire that it would bring. She imagined Eli alive and safe, completely soaked in a downpour. Then she spread that sensation to other creatures in the forest, trees, blackberry brambles, vines, and all other life.

All around her, the Leekins unified by holding hands while buzzing in the air and closing their eyes tightly, imagining the same rain. Their hearts flowed with love of the forest and the intense urge to protect it from ruin. They sang:

> *We are the Leekins*
> *Full of love and respect.*
> *Let the rain take its effect*
> *And give us clear instruction*
> *To protect our home from destruction!*

Suddenly, the smell of rain filled the air, just as Sarah had been imagining. Sarah was not sure if the smell was real or still in her imagination until she felt cool drops bathing her fur. The smell of woodsmoke and heat singeing her nose rapidly faded. She morphed back into human form yet again, feeling safe enough to be herself. She had already come close to defeating Madras, a feat she had not believed herself capable of until now. Her heart swelled with pride, and her eyes brimmed with tears.

She turned to the sound of someone running into the clearing. It was Eli. Though he looked sooty, and his hair was burned, he was in one piece. Dripping wet, he ran to her and seized her.

"Are you okay?" he demanded.

Sarah burst into happy tears and pulled away to survey Eli. "I'll do alright! You're the one I was worried about, not me!"

Jenna ran up and threw her arms around Eli's neck. "I thought for sure you were dead!" she cried. She buried her face into his chest, sobbing. Eli awkwardly patted her back, looking at Sarah uncomfortably.

"Wait!" Eli froze when he saw Madras. He shrank back in terror when he noticed that she was the evil lookalike of Lativia. "Is that . . . Madras?" His voice was full of horrified awe.

During Sarah's spell chanting, Lativia and Daisy had seized the moment to cast Madras in a freezing spell together. They now stood together in the center of the clearing, flanked by ghosts who looked angry at all that Madras had done to disturb their peace atop

Mount Katribus. Madras did not move, rooted as she was to her spot. Addie and Kelvin were circling her paralyzed spirit body, eyeing her fiercely, sure to lunge if Madras attempted to escape or attack Lativia again.

Though Madras was frozen in place, she could still speak. She glared at Lativia, and began to slowly utter a spell in a ghastly, hateful voice. A flash of green energy spewed out of her mouth and into the air, headed straight for Lativia.

Addie lunged into the air, soaring through and then over the magic. With her weight, she bowled into Madras, sending her crashing to the ground. Kelvin lunged on top of her as well, pinning her to the ground completely. She groaned with the heaviness of the two wolves on her chest.

Madras broke apart into her many factions once again, and they began to mutter another green death spell in unison.

"No!" Sarah threw out her palm and deflected the spell, sending it zinging off into the trees, where it dissipated.

Madras's spirits joined back together again, and she looked pale and frightened. She knew that she had been defeated. Lativia ran forward and towered over her, but then hesitated, uncertain what to do. Though she was a powerful witch, she also clearly was confused by her love for her sister. She did not want to do anything to hurt Madras, and neither did Kelvin or Addie. Terrified of what this pause could allow Madras to do, Sarah ran to stand over her as well, ready to deflect any other spells she might attempt to unleash.

Fortunately, the Leekins had finished casting fire-retardant spells over the forest and rushed to the rescue. Clover Figcreek and the other Leekins instantly began to form a ring in the air above Madras, chanting:

> *Earth bring forth*
> *Vines and roots, headed north!*
> *Come quick, come strong*
> *We can't wait long!*

Vines and roots coated in ghostly blue light shot out of the earth, lashing around Madras's legs and arms, restraining her completely. "Now you won't go anywhere or practice any magic!" Clover Figcreek cried triumphantly. "You are officially defeated!"

As Madras fought against the enchanted vegetal restraints, they refused to give. She began to howl in rage and frustration. "Let me go!" she screamed. She looked over at Levi, who had stood still through all of the magical action, his mouth agape. "Free me, you fool!" she screamed at him.

But Levi did nothing. He simply stared at the dark

witch, clearly stunned. Blood was spreading down his leg, but he did not appear to notice it anymore.

"You are hereby banished from Witchland!" Jenna shouted at the top of her lungs. "You may not cross the gate any longer with your magic!" Jenna began to recite a gatekeeper incantation that made the color completely leave Madras's already pale form.

The gate is closed
From dangers who pose!
A threat to be banned
I hereby command!

"No," Madras sobbed. "You have to believe me. I'm not the sister you need to banish! Banish her!" She fixed her eyes on Lativia, and they roiled with loathing.

"I wish that were true," Lativia said, her voice heavy with grief. "I love you, Madras. I always have. And it kills me that I must treat you as an enemy, but that is the choice you made, not I."

"No, you don't love me or feel a bit sorry for all of this!" Madras spat between sobs that wracked her ghostly body. "You hate me! You abandoned me to die!"

"Because of your dabbling in the dark arts, I could not save you." Lativia began to cry as well. "I wanted to save you. I really did. It killed me to leave you there at the stake, dying in agony; you have no idea. I carried that to my grave, my broken heart, and I feel it every day."

"Then why didn't you save me, if you loved me that much?" Madras implored.

"We just couldn't bite through your ropes when you were already sharing your body with demons. You chose the evil path, and your demons would not let us wolves near," Lativia replied. "They wanted you to die, so that they could take over your spirit and live on forever."

"I chose a path! That doesn't make me evil!" Madras argued. "I was promised great things, and I have accomplished them."

"Roaming New England woods, living in caves deep underground, enticing humans to join you on the dark side and do your dirty work against me." Lativia shook her head. "You have hurt many people in your wolf form. And in your spirit form. You have not accomplished anything but evil with your chosen path. And what a lonely life you lead! Without even a coven to love you."

"You sure brought a lot of harm to Witchland in a short time," Sarah admonished Madras. "If you weren't evil, you would not have done that. I'm sure you feel wronged, but we can't let you free. You are not good for this town, and you need to stay away, forever."

"I curse you!" Madras spat. But, contained within her new restraints cast by the gatekeeper and the Leekins, she was also powerless, unable to exercise her dark magic on anyone or anything. "I will find a way back in! I always will!"

"And we will find a way to defeat you, as we always do," Daisy replied calmly.

"I hereby banish you from these woods forever," Clover Figcreek declared. The defiant shrill in her voice indicated her deep pride at finally vanquishing the dark witch who had gotten the best of her and her kind this time, preventing them from doing their jobs as protectors of the forest.

With this declaration, Madras vanished, her bound ghost now somewhere far from Witchland, where she could no longer harm them.

"Where did you send her?" Sarah asked Clover Figcreek.

"I have no control over where she went," Clover Figcreek replied. She dusted her hands together, clearly satisfied with her work. "All I know is she isn't here anymore!"

The other Leekins cheered and gathered around Clover Figcreek in celebration.

"I have to make a new deed if we can't find the old one," Lativia vowed. "I can't let this happen again." Then she turned away, trying to hide her deep grief over what had just happened and the long, ugly past she had shared with her sister.

Addie hurried to Sarah's side. A bit of Madras's magic had hit her and affected her like a bullet, leaving a streak of blood down Addie's side. Sarah knelt beside her and petted her. "I'm going to make you some of that healing potion when we reach the bottom of the mountain," she assured Addie.

"I had to protect you and save the town," Addie answered. *"Did I do a good job?"*

"You are *such* a good girl," Sarah told her. She rubbed behind Addie's ears, Addie's favorite spot. "By the way, your friend Kelvin over there looks like he wants to talk to you." Sarah eyed Kelvin, who had slunk back into the trees around the clearing but was still circling, watching Addie. He appeared to have a few minor injuries as well and walked with a limp.

"He doesn't like such a large crowd," Addie told her. *"I'll be right back."* She ran off to join Kelvin. The two loped off into the woods, though Sarah knew they weren't going far. They were going to lick each other's wounds and help heal each other. The love of wolves was as strong as humans, and even more loyal.

No longer under Madras's dark spell, Levi turned toward Rick, Jenna, Daisy, and Sarah, who were standing there, shell-shocked by the action that had just transpired. "I—I don't even know what just happened. I can't believe all of this. . . ." With a deep groan of shock, he ran his fingers through his hair, looking around him in disbelief.

"Were you under Madras's spell?" Sarah asked him.

He nodded slowly. "I think so. I didn't want to do anything like this, not at all. I came for some closure with my brother. I didn't mean to get dragged into all of this."

"Do you confess to the murder of the town clerk?" Eli demanded, his hand on the handcuffs linked to his belt.

"The murder? What murder? No, no, I didn't kill anyone," Levi replied hastily, backing away from Eli with his hands up in the air. "Please don't arrest me for that. I am not a murderer."

"Then why did you send ten grand to Mayor Lewis?" Sarah asked. "And why were you texting him about payments?"

Levi shook his head, clearly bewildered by these accusations. "What on earth are you talking about?"

"You don't remember me catching you texting someone called ML in your phone? When you were staying in the abandoned house?" Sarah began to doubt that Levi had even been himself at that time. He certainly seemed disoriented and genuinely baffled by their accusations.

"He was possessed by Madras to act as her physical errand boy in Witchland," Daisy spoke up, her voice grim. "He doesn't remember a thing that he did."

Sarah and Eli exchanged disappointed looks. "We still have no case," Eli said, disappointment evident in his voice and the firm set of his jaw.

"Who was murdered? Did I do it?" Levi's voice wavered as he looked from Sarah to Eli and back again.

"The wolf hairs had Mayor Lewis's life energy in them," Daisy spoke up again. "When I analyzed them, I found only his energy, not anyone else's. Levi is not the one who killed Mr. Atticos. At least, not directly."

"Not directly?" Levi's voice had a despairing edge to it as he clutched his face in horror. "I wanted revenge. I wanted something. But when a beautiful woman came to me in my dreams and said I could have it all back and vindicate my brother, I didn't expect this. I didn't agree to kill anyone!"

"Madras took control of you in your moment of weakness and tempted you with a promise of vindication and closure. You wanted revenge, so you gave her an easy way into your heart and your mind. Don't feel guilty," Daisy reassured him gently. "You're not responsible for this. You just allowed yourself to be used as a pawn by Madras, which is what she does best. I have heard tales of her doing such things all over New England to get her evil work done for her."

"But what did I actually do?" Levi demanded.

No one could answer. "We're not sure exactly what," Sarah finally told him. "I think you played a hand in bribing someone else to murder somebody. I think Madras wasn't able to completely convince you to kill Mr. Atticos and steal the deed yourself, so you used your own money to hire Mayor Lewis to do it."

Levi let out an anguished sob. "I am so sorry," he told the air, as if addressing Mr. Atticos. Then he buried his face in his hands and his shoulders shook with his guilty sobs.

"But why would Mayor Lewis do this? Was he possessed by Madras, too?" Sarah mused to the cops. "And if so, why did Levi need to get involved at all?"

"You would be surprised what some of the nicest people are capable of," Jenna replied grimly. "We see it all of the time as cops. The nice ones, the ones you would never suspect, are always the ones you really need to watch out for."

"The bribe," Sarah suddenly gasped, thinking of the money in his account. "He was willing to kill someone for ten thousand dollars. But why? Why not just steal the document?"

"I'll tell you what happened to me," said a new voice.

Everyone turned to see the town clerk's ghost standing there behind them.

CHAPTER TEN

"Mr. Atticos!" everyone gasped. In the fray
of the fight with Madras, they had failed to consider he
might be here, among the ghosts that dwelled on
Mount Katribus.

"My name is Peter," the clerk began in a trembling
voice. "Call—call me Peter." He swallowed, trying to
get his stutter under control. "Sorry if I'm a bit shaky.
I'm still upset about being killed. I wasn't ready to die,
not yet."

"I'm sorry," Sarah began, overwhelmed with grief
at the sight of the ghost. Like Michael, his life was cut
short when he was not ready. The sense of tragedy and
sadness around him was so thick that it choked her.
Her heart bled for him and the wretched look on his
face.

"Don't say sorry," he cut her off, holding his hand

up. "All you can do is hear my story and make things right. Bring justice to my death, please."

"Of course," Eli said, stepping forward. He appeared as shocked and overcome as Sarah had been the first time she had come to this clearing and encountered Michael's ghost. "We will do whatever we can to put your killer behind bars."

"It was Mayor Lewis," Peter went on. Then his eyes widened. "He betrayed me. He really betrayed me." The anguish of his betrayal was apparent in his voice. "I thought he was at least something of a friend. I had no idea how shallow of a friend he really was!"

"Why would he kill you?" Eli demanded, his jaw set. Like any cop, he liked learning the truth, but he also had to understand every detail. He was already attempting to figure out how to gather evidence and prosecute Mayor Lewis, considering the testimony of a ghost would not hold up too well in court.

"Money and the threat to his power." Peter shrugged. "He was hard up on cash, that much I know. And he was pretty threatened by Sarah here. When it was just Daisy and Hua and Margaret, well, he could handle that. Some eccentric women in the woods, making potions in their little hex houses, as he put it, was fine enough by him. They could be ignored, controlled even if they got too out of hand. But with Sarah's entrance to the town drama, he realized that

Witchland was becoming a powerful haven of witches once again. He didn't like that. It scared him. Especially with the town's history, you know, Madras's wolf attacks in the forest in the 1600s."

"But we would never do anything like that," Sarah interjected, her heart sinking. The evident prejudice against her kind was becoming more and more obvious the longer she was a witch. She hated the idea that people were so ignorant about what witches really were. She was also dismayed by the danger her kind faced from persecution.

Eli placed a comforting hand on her back. Daisy just sighed and said, "You learn to live with the hatred, my dear."

"Why did he kill you, though? And what did Levi Gonforth have to do with all of this?" Eli wondered.

"I'll tell you, he came to town to find out what had really happened with his brother," Peter explained. "You know, he thought maybe John was wrongly framed or something. He didn't believe the charges. But the inn was full, so he was staying a few towns over. Then he was enchanted by Madras in his sleep, through a dream. You know, that woman apparently really got to his head. Madras knew she couldn't get into Witchland with the deed there, so she had to use people to do her dirty work for her.

"Levi got so excited and wanted to avenge his

brother. He learned he could do so by weakening the town, but first he needed to get to the deed. He came to my office one night and tried to break in. He didn't even realize I was in there—working late, as I liked to do. I scared him off with a baseball bat. He knew after that he needed someone to help him on the inside, so he approached Mayor Lewis, promising him money and a way to bring down the witches of Witchland.

"I didn't know any of this at the time, of course. I was just in my office the next night, feeling uneasy, keeping an eye out for the thief." Peter sighed heavily, the memory agonizing for him to recall. "That's when I heard a weird noise in the hallway. A wolf growl, deep and low. I grabbed my baseball bat and hurried out there to get him. I thought it was the thief, you know, trying to distract me. But I saw a strange-looking wolf in the hallway, and I chased him out to the alley. He tried to run from me, but I knew there was something wrong with him, that he wasn't a real wolf. I thought he must be Madras herself, since she likes to freak people out by turning into a wolf. So, I went after it attempting to stun it with my bat, and it attacked me, and I know wolves don't attack people. Just like that, I realized I was standing outside of my body and—and I was dead." Peter let out a strangled sob and covered his face with his hands.

"It was a demon wolf after all?" Eli said, sounding

disappointed but also relieved in the same breath. Sarah realized how much he needed convincing that it was a demon wolf behind the attack.

"No. Remember, wolves are good. It was Mayor Lewis transformed into a wolf," Daisy spoke up. "He took a bad shapeshifting potion—I recognized the signs of his withdrawal when he came to visit me. I'm sure Madras had Levi make it up and offer it to him to help him scare Peter off and get into the office safe more easily."

"I swear, I wasn't aware of any of this," Levi stressed. "I don't even believe—I didn't believe in magic."

Peter laughed. "Oh, yes, it was Mayor Lewis all right. Because as I stood there, watching him maul my body, he already started to change back to human form. Then I heard someone running out of the town hall. This man"—Peter pointed at Levi, who stood looking horrified—"had used Mayor Lewis's keys to grab the deed out of the safe. That and the money, which he used to pay Mayor Lewis with later. You see, I watched all of this for a few days before coming up here. I had to make sense of what was going on, what was happening to the deed."

"What did happen to the deed?" asked Lativia.

"Levi burned it," Peter said. "Took it outside of the town's limits and burned it. Then the town's defenses crumbled, and Madras was allowed right in. All of this pain and betrayal and evil, just so Madras could own Witchland and vanquish her sister. You know that's been her goal all along, but this time was her closest to successful attempt."

"Sadly, that is what my sister does," Lativia said gravely. She walked over to Peter. "I am terribly sorry for how you died, but now you're here with us. You will learn that being a spirit is not so bad." She placed a loving hand on Peter's forehead. "It is peaceful. You need not work; just enjoy the enchanted wine and food of our feasts."

"I think I am ready to cross over," Peter said wearily. "I just had to tell *someone* my story. But now that I have, I just want to rest—I'm old."

"Come," Lativia told him, leading him away from the living humans in the clearing. "We will discuss this more." They began to fade into the gloomy air, without even a goodbye.

"Um, where did they go?" Eli asked tremulously.

"It's a ghost thing," Sarah explained to him. "They don't stay in this realm too long for us to see and converse with them. This clearing is one of the few places where the veil between the other side and this world is thin enough that we can meet for a while. Of course, the Leekins and animal familiars can always see the dead, at all times."

"That's right. But now it's time for you all to go home," Clover Figcreek spoke up petulantly. "We are tired, and we need our sleep. You humans are always here at the oddest hours, bothering us, never respecting the sacredness of rest!"

"Well," said Eli slowly. "I've never taken testimony from a ghost, but there's a first for everything. Now I just have to figure out how to make this stand up in court."

"We'll find a way," Jenna assured him. "We did with John and Dismas, so we will again."

Sarah looked around for Michael and Aunt Beth. They both stepped forward, sensing her call, and hugged her. Then they, too, began to fade away into the air. A stillness fell over the clearing as the ghosts vanished, one by one. Eli watched with his mouth hanging open, never having seen anything like this before.

The humans left on the mountain began to slowly hike back down to the village.

CHAPTER ELEVEN

Just as Sarah woke up in the morning and set about feeding Addie, who had finally come home around midnight from her foray with Kelvin, she heard a gentle rap on her door. Thinking it must be Hua and Margaret, she opened it. To her surprise, Jenna stood on her doorstep, holding Lativia's spellbook.

"I picked this up for you. You forgot it in all of the action up there last night," she said.

"Thanks!" Sarah smiled as she accepted the book. Its weight made her lean forward slightly. Sensing that Jenna had more to say, Sarah welcomed her inside.

Jenna hesitated for a second but then came in. She sat on the edge of the couch in the client meeting room —or so-called living room—looking uncomfortable. "Listen, I'm not one to beat around the bush, so let me get right to it. I want you to know that I like you. And I think you and I make a great team. We all have to work together to protect this town. It's one of the last of its kind, and everyone wants to take it over, to destroy it, to control it. Our collective job as Witchlanders is to defend it."

"I agree." Sarah nodded. "I'm always going to do my best, and I really appreciate all of your help."

"I have to admit . . . I didn't totally like you at first. That's because, well, I envied you." Jenna shifted, clearly embarrassed. "I have to confess something. . . ."

"That you're in love with Eli," Sarah finished for her.

Jenna looked taken aback, then ashamed. "It's that obvious, huh?"

"Pretty obvious to me looking in, but I don't think Eli has a clue." Sarah thought back to Eli's uncomfortable expression last night on the mountain, when Jenna had hugged him tightly and sobbed with relief into his chest. Maybe he did believe Sarah now, that Jenna liked him.

"Well, I can tell that you have a thing for him, too, and I can also tell he likes you back," Jenna said.

"How can you tell?" Sarah flushed and felt her heart begin beating frantically.

"I know my partner pretty well. It's obvious in the way he talks about you, the way he looks at you. He's smitten." She gave a weak chuckle. "It hurts me, but I also just want Eli to be happy. And I don't want to make an enemy out of you over jealousy."

"I don't want that either," Sarah said vehemently.

"So, if Eli wants to be with you, and you want to be with him, then don't waste any time. You two should be together. I think you'd make a great couple," Jenna went on.

Sarah laughed. "I'm so bad with men. I don't have a clue what I'm doing."

"Then let Eli lead you. He's been hurt badly. His ex-wife really did a number on him. He needs to feel comfortable before moving forward, but when he's ready, he will make the first move," Jenna explained. "That's the kind of guy he is, very take-charge, very strong."

Sarah realized she had been holding her breath and let it out in a woosh. "I will let him make the first move, but I want to encourage him somehow. Do you have any ideas?"

"This feels plain old weird telling you how to get the man of my dreams." Jenna groaned and began to rub her eyes with the heels of her hands. "Just be there for him, be sweet to him, talk to him every day. He will come around soon enough. He loves it when you text him and ask him how his day was; keep that up."

"Thank you." Sarah got up and wrapped her arms around Jenna in a warm hug. "I'm sorry," she added.

"Just promise me you won't hurt him." Jenna gazed up at Sarah with her brown eyes blazing passionately. "I can't bear to see him hurt."

"I will never hurt him," Sarah assured her.

Jenna left shortly after, and Sarah felt dazed as she finished mixing up Addie's homemade food. She felt bad for Jenna, but also giddy with delight that Eli liked her back. Not only had she defeated Madras, but she may have found the love of her life.

"I just want to thank you," Hua said as Sarah handed her a thumbtack. She pressed the thumbtack into the telephone pole, pinning up a sign that read, 'Make this witch the mayor of Witchland!'

"For what?" Sarah asked.

"For saving the town. And for clearing our names. Daisy was getting the worst of it, but when these witch hunts start—we all become victims," Hua said sadly. "After all, we are all in this together."

Sarah beamed. "I couldn't have done it without you all! I had a whole team to support me. And the spells you taught me, and that healing potion recipe you shared with me? They really helped."

Hua smiled. "Addie is all healed up now?"

"All healed up and in love with some forest wolf

named Kelvin," Sarah replied. She smiled warmly, thinking of her best canine friend.

"That's cute," Hua said. "We all need love!"

"Yoo-hoo!" someone called. The two witches turned to see Daisy, waving them over to Javacadabra. They meandered over to join her, and she welcomed them inside for tea.

"What an adventure these past few days have been," Daisy said as she stirred honey into her cup of tea. "Mayor Lewis in prison, Madras banished far away, and now we're all working on a new deed to the town for Lativia to enchant."

"I think it's almost finished," Sarah said. "Jenna is checking it for 'loopholes.' I made sure it's up to par with paranormal law."

"It even looks like the old one. Margaret spilled tea on the edges of the paper to give it that old-timey look," Hua told Daisy.

Daisy grinned. "The town will be protected from evil once again. I can sleep easier now."

"Evil will still try to find its way in, but I think we have a pretty good defense team assembled here." Hua winked at Sarah. "We'll all have to work together as usual to keep trouble out."

Sarah grinned back. "I am going to keep learning and practicing every day," she vowed. "I can't let myself get complacent."

"No, never get complacent. There is always plenty to learn with magic. You can never learn it all," Daisy agreed. "After all, I'm about to be sixty, and I am still learning."

"Same here." Hua nodded. "New potions, new herbs I didn't even know existed before. Did you know they just found a new plant in the Amazon that can cure cancer? I can't wait to get some of it and start making cancer-curing potions. I have a friend with breast cancer, and I think we can cure it." She grinned, clearly ecstatic.

"What's this about a witch for mayor, by the way?" Susie teased Hua, coming over to their table for a moment. "Do you really think this town will elect you?"

"I don't know if they'll vote for me specifically, but I think we can remove the stigma surrounding witches. After all, convicting Mayor Lewis cleared Daisy's name, and witches are no longer so unpopular around here," Hua said optimistically. "If I am public about who I am, maybe public opinion will become even more positive."

"A magically inclined lesbian mayor." Susie grinned. "We have come so far. I don't doubt you could win."

"That's the idea, anyway. Every minority has had a civil rights movement. Now we need to stage ours,"

Sarah added. "Magical pride."

Daisy looked doubtful. "I don't know about the prejudice lifting in my lifetime. I have always lived with prejudice, from the time I was a baby. But our work makes things easier for future generations, at least. All I can say is thank you. Thank you for believing in me and clearing my name, Sarah."

"I knew you didn't do it!" Sarah told her. "I *had* to clear your name. But it wasn't just me that did that. You certainly helped. You were brave enough to accompany me to the top of the mountain when I was paralyzingly scared."

"You both did it," Hua chimed in, raising her cup of tea in a toast.

"*We* all did it," Sarah corrected her. Then she raised her own cup, and the five witches toasted. "To Witchland!" they cheered.

Sarah's phone vibrated with a text. "Uh-oh, it's Eli," she said. "I hope there hasn't been another murder." She said this in half jest, but she was still slightly apprehensive as she opened the message.

"Want to meet for lunch today?" the message read.

Hua, Susie, and Daisy watched Sarah with affectionate amusement as she flushed red. "Sure!" Sarah texted Eli back.

"Mr. Handsome?" Daisy teased.

"Eli," Sarah replied. Then she noticed the looks on their faces. "Shut up! He's handsome."

"That he is," the three witches agreed.

"Do you finally have a date?" Hua asked.

"Just lunch. I kind of want to go home and change into something cuter, though," Sarah told them.

"Do it. He obviously cares about you, too," Daisy urged her.

Sarah rushed home and changed into her favorite dress that was not too light for the mildly chilly afternoon. She brushed her hair, added some mascara to her lashes and a dash of lipstick to her lips, and slipped on her new flat sandals. Then she met Eli back at Javacadabra, where he hugged her. Hua and Daisy were now gone, and Susie watched them with teasing amusement from behind the espresso machine, where she pretended to be cleaning, when really, she was eavesdropping on their conversation.

"Wow, you—you look nice," he complimented her.

She beamed. "So do you." She loved the way he looked in his crisp uniform.

They settled into a booth with veggie cream cheese sandwiches and tea lattes. Through the window, Sarah could see that Daisy and Hua were still conversing over tea in the apothecary.

"I heard you made an arrest," Sarah said. "How did you guys figure that one out?"

"We had a saliva sample, and the crime lab matched it to Mayor Lewis's. Of course, the hair didn't match, so the DA prosecution is going to say he planted it there, the fur and the wolf prints, in an attempt to cover up what he did and blame it on an innocent animal. Combined with the fact he didn't sign out till after the murder that night, and he had the exact amount missing from the safe in his bank account, we have a pretty good case against him," Eli answered.

"Congratulations to you and Jenna. Two murders solved in a short time." She sighed. "I just wish this violence didn't have to happen for us to protect this place. I just wish we could have some peace."

"I have to admit, what happened on top of that mountain . . . my mind is still blown." Eli shook his head, blowing out his cheeks. "The stuff we don't think is real actually is."

"It threw me for a loop when I first went up there, too," Sarah agreed.

"You were awesome up there," he complimented her. The softness and admiration in his eyes was unmistakable.

"I couldn't have done it alone. We work best in a coven," she joked.

He laughed nervously. "Then, I'm glad you have your coven. Your coven can help the Witchland police department anytime."

"Thanks. I like being a detective." Sarah laughed.

Just then, Harriet breezed into the shop, wearing her pointy hat as always and with Edgar roosting on her shoulder. "Aww, Sarah and Eli, sittin' in a tree," she sang before cackling.

Sarah rolled her eyes and pretended to be very interested in her food to hide her blush. Eli also shifted in his seat, looking embarrassed. They were both relieved when Harriet finally left, carrying a bag of zucchini muffins that she began to pick apart and feed to Edgar in front of the shop.

"*I don't like that bird,*" Zeva the cat remarked coolly from the counter, where she laid in her bed.

They chatted and finished their lunches. Then Eli's radio went off, alerting him that a raccoon was inside a residence and he needed to get it out. He sighed as he stood up. "I guess I have to take care of this. At least I got to finish lunch this time."

"I'm glad we got to eat, too," Sarah said.

Eli paused, surveying Sarah. "Speaking of eating, I was wondering . . . now that everything's slowed down and all . . . dinner . . . maybe?" Eli shoved his hands in his pockets, looking like a shy teenage boy for a second.

Sarah smiled. "It's a date, Officer Eli."

She dodged Susie's overeager smile and walked home. There, she noticed that her mother had called her while she was eating with Eli. She returned the call, planning how much she would tell her parents and how much she would leave out. While she did not want to terrify them with tales of her encounter with her evil ancestor, she also felt they should know she was embracing her Spellwood abilities.

"Hi, honey," her mother answered the phone.

"What are you doing?" Sarah asked, settling in her rocking chair while Addie lay down at her feet. She observed the birds in her yard, pecking at seed that had fallen from the feeder she kept brimming for them.

"Oh, just painting. A seascape, actually. Your father is reading one of his law books. We're just enjoying a lazy day," her mother said cheerily.

"I suppose that's what you get to do after you retire." Sarah laughed. "I've been . . . quite busy."

"That's good! I didn't think you would have much to do in that little town."

"Actually . . . there's a lot more to do here than I expected." Sarah scratched the back of her calf with her toe. "Um, I have to tell you something, Mom."

Her mother was silent in expectation.

"I'm . . . well, you know how I'm a Spellwood," Sarah began awkwardly.

Her mother sighed heavily. "I knew it."

"You knew what?" Sarah moved to the edge of her rocking chair, her heart hammering in her throat. This confession to her parents was more nerve-wracking than she had imagined.

"Don't think I have forgotten the way you used to talk to that goat at your aunt Beth's farm, and bring back just the right herbs for her potions without being told what to pick. And don't think I don't notice how you see ghosts or your eerie intuition. Honey, it's in your blood, and your father's, too. Just because we don't like to talk about it in our family doesn't mean we are completely blind to it." Her mother sighed again. "The truth is we really just wanted to protect you. People hate witches."

"They hate lawyers, too, but you wanted me to be a lawyer," Sarah joked.

"They don't burn lawyers at the stake," her mother chided. "We just wanted you to . . . to have a normal childhood. To feel like you fit in at school. And to not be persecuted."

Sarah swallowed and nodded, overcome with love and admiration for her parents. "Please tell me you're not angry that I've embraced my powers?"

"Angry, no. Worried, yes," her mother said softly. "I just don't want people to go after you."

"I promise you, I'm very discreet. Except to a few people who know about the magic that abounds here, anyway," Sarah assured her.

Her mother sounded relieved. "Would you like to talk to your father now?"

"Yes, I want to hear his take," Sarah agreed.

But her father spoke up in the background, "I heard enough of Darlene's side of the conversation to know what you're about to tell me, baby girl. I figured as much would happen when you moved to that little town. Don't forget, I grew up there. I know what it's about." He gave a small laugh. "As long as you're being careful and discreet, I don't mind. I just want you to be happy."

"Did you ever see the Leekins?" Sarah asked.

"Those annoying little things." Her father groaned. Then he and Sarah both laughed.

———

Sarah and Eli sat together near the large outdoor fireplace on the patio of Geno's Ristorante Italiano, tucking into a plate of spaghetti and nibbling on delicious garlic bread. From the patio, they could view the whole town square, lit up by the rising moon.

"This chardonnay is really good, really buttery. I have to check out this 'Noisy Creek' winery." Sarah surveyed the label on the bottle, trying to make light conversation to hide how flustered she was from the romantic atmosphere of their date. A candle flickered next to the wine bottle in its bucket of ice, and soft jazz played over the patio speakers. The last time she had been on such a nice date had been for her nine-year wedding anniversary with Jeff.

"You deserve it, all of it, after all you've done and the stress of what happened up there." Eli indicated Mount Katribus, its peak standing tall over the town. There was no need to repeat what had happened—it would sound looney if they ever spoke of it out loud again. "We both need to just let the recent events slip out of our minds."

Sarah had been longing to see Eli in candlelight, or firelight. He was even more handsome with parts of his face submerged in the flickering shadows. She had also never seen him so relaxed before. "This is how you separate work and your personal life? By eating Italian?" she teased.

"Not normally, but it is now that I have someone to eat with." He laughed.

Sarah blushed.

"Ah, look, she's blushing," Addie heckled from the floor, where she was cuddled with Kelvin. The two looked made for each other, despite the wolf's considerably greater size and wilder look. Sarah had cast them both in a camouflage spell so that they could join her and Eli at the Italian restaurant. She was not sure how the town would react to the presence of a large

wild wolf walking around and entering dining establishments, and with so much misinformation about wolves abounding in the public, she did not want to risk it.

"*I hope he doesn't have mange,*" Sarah teased Addie telepathically.

Kelvin glared at her. "*I'm very clean actually, thank you very much.*"

"*I gave him a good tongue bath earlier,*" Addie added indignantly.

"Are they making fun of us?" With a wry smile, Eli asked carefully. Though he did not have the ability to hear their words as Sarah did, he knew they spoke freely to her.

"Oh, you have no idea." Sarah placed a hand on top of Eli's. "They're happy right now. And so am I." She felt bold doing this, and also good. Maybe making a small move would help coax Eli to make a bigger one.

He glanced at her hand, smiling. "I have to admit, we make a great team."

"A cop and a witch? The Salem Witch Trial crowd must be rolling in their graves right now!" Sarah joked.

A log fell in the fireplace and erupted in a loud crackle of sparks. Both Eli and Sarah jumped, then laughed when they realized where the noise came from. Eli held out his arm, and Sarah snuggled into the comfortable crook of his shoulder, drinking in his manly warmth and the security of being near him. His cologne smelled heavenly.

"Maybe things will calm down now," Sarah said happily.

"We can only hope," Eli replied. But there was a tinge of doubt in his voice.

"Either way, I sense we will be just fine," Sarah added after a reflective pause.

"Of course. You are a Spellwood, and I am a Strongheart! Remember that," Eli reminded her.

Sarah glanced up at him, overcome with gratitude to know him. Without intending to, she started to tell him the story of her ex-husband, who had walked out on her without any explanation. Tears sparked in her eyes. "Since then . . . I haven't dated anyone. Or even thought about it. But you . . . you made me believe that I could be loved again."

Eli stared down at her. Then, suddenly, he cupped her chin in his hand and pulled her face close to place a gentle kiss on her lips.

Behind her eyes, sparks erupted. As Eli gently pulled away, Sarah placed her hand on the back of his head and pulled him back in to kiss longer. She relished the taste of his lips and the tickle of his beard stubble on her chin.

Addie and Kelvin cooed at her from the floor and commenced licking each other as well.

Sarah knew in her heart that everything in her life was coming together, and she now only had to enjoy her fresh start. She would take this over the immense power Madras had offered her any day. There was so much more power in being good than evil in the end.

Curious how the magic of a crow's tail can help Sarah and Addie save Witchland?

Get Tail of a Feather Now

http://getbook.at/tailofafeather

A NOTE FROM MELANIE

Ms. Addie Pants loves her ball when not solving mysteries with Sarah.

Thanks so much for reading this book. I love how the wisdom and magic of wolves help Sarah and Addie solve the crime at hand. Don't you?

This story was near and dear to my heart as a wolf biologist. But wolves are also my spirit animal. Everyday they guide me to be a better human.

But lynx and wolves are not the only spirit animals for Sarah to discover. Check out the next book.

Stay tuned for a sneak preview of the third book in the series, Tail of a Feather, which is now available on Amazon. https://getbook.at/tailofafeather. Thanks again.

With Beautiful Magic,
    Melanie Snow and Addie

PS: Reviews help authors keep writing. Please feel free to leave one!

As the clues fly, Sarah is shocked to learn that Madras Spellwood is trying to get back into Witchland to take over its beauty and magic. But Sarah and Addie are vowed defenders of the forest, and they will not let Madras succeed, or Eli get away.

Can Sarah save Eli and beat Madras at the same time?

Tail of a Feather is the third book in the magical Spellwood Witches cozy mystery series. If you like paranormal puzzles, charming canine companions, and a bit of flirty romance, then you will love Melanie Snow's crafty quest.

Buy Tail of a Feather and take flight into the magical world of Witchland today!

http://getbook.at/tailofafeather

ENJOY AN EXCERPT FROM TAIL OF A FEATHER

Do you want to know what happens to Sarah and Addie as they continue on their quest? Or what about the eight crows that appear to challenge Sarah: will she succeed? You will be able to find out in the next book of the series:Tail of a Feather!

Tail of a Feather is now available on Amazon. Download your copy right now! http://getbook.at/tailofafeather

Not ready to get your own copy? Enjoy part of the first chapter for free on the next page!

Chapter 1

Tail of a Feather, Book 3 of The Spellwood Witches

What on earth is all that noise? Sarah cracked her eyes open, disgruntled at being woken from her lovely dream of Eli Strongheart, police chief of Witchland, New Hampshire, and the love of her life, feeding her tiramisu in a candlelit restaurant. The romantic violin serenade in her dream had been disrupted by the distinct sound of Addie barking fervently and—

Are those crows cawing?

Sarah's eyes flew wide open, and she turned her head to observe her familiar, Addie, standing before the bay window in the bedroom, wagging her tail and making enough noise to keep Sarah from falling off to sleep again. But Addie was not facing out the window; she was staring intently at Sarah, trying to wake her up.

"What is it, girl?" Sarah asked, swinging her legs out from under the cozy cover and cringing when her bare feet touched the cold floor. She located her slippers and strode up to the window. It let in only some feeble light, telling Sarah it was barely dawn. "It's early. This had better be important," Sarah grumbled.

"*The crows! They're telling us something!*" Addie replied, jumping up and down in excitement now that she had successfully roused her person. "*They keep saying, 'Danger! Danger!'*"

Sarah stared down into the big maple tree that stood in front of her house. Its branches were heavily laden with shiny black crows, beaks open and wings flapping with the effort of their raucous chorus. While Sarah had often seen one or two crows in the woods and heard their croaks and caws, she had never seen such a large murder.

"*It's about time they got here!*" Addie barked. "*It's already six-thirty in the morning—and they say they just got here! For dog biscuits' sake, if they were ravens, they would have been here sooner. Can we call upon the ravens instead?*"

"What are you going on about?" Sarah demanded. "Why did they need to get here? Did they have an appointment?" She said the last part in jest. As a real estate attorney, she often received clients in the little front room of the cottage where she lived in Witchland, New Hampshire, though never this early and never of the bird variety. She had inherited both the cottage and the law practice from her law school mentor and longtime friend, Michael Howler. In return, she had solved Michael's murder and brought justice and peace to his ghost, as well as the town of Witchland.

"*Sarah, you remember what Lativia, the greatest witch of all time, told us about seeing eight crows? Don't you?*" Addie stared at Sarah intently with her large brown eyes, wagging her tail with expectation.

Sarah racked her brain. "She says so many things, and her messages are all insanely cryptic. I can't think right now, Addie."

"*Your noble ancestor was extremely clear that they would be bearers of an important message and that they would signal bad news that you need to attend to,*" Addie said, a slight nip of impatience in her voice.

Sarah's eyes widened as the conversation with the ghost of her revered witch ancestor came back to her with vivid clarity. "Yes, of course. Now I remember she told us something about eight crows and about a slew of important questions, how they would be key to solving our next mystery in our town of Witchland," Sarah replied.

"*Well, I guess something bad happened last night and they just now got here,*" Addie said with annoyance.

Just then, one of the crows flew onto the flower box in front of Sarah's living room windows and began to peck frantically at the glass. The loud tapping sound filled the house. The other crows began to caw even more loudly, and Sarah worried they were disturbing her neighbors, Margaret and Hua, who were always up this early tending to their massive greenhouse and many gardens.

"Let's go down there and see what the message is," Addie prompted. *"We can't waste a minute. It has to do with Eli; I can just tell by their caws."*

Panic gripped Sarah's chest. She hastily threw on her coat to guard against the deep fall chill and chased her familiar outside. Her nose burned in the cold as she and Addie looked up toward the earsplitting sounds.

Within the branches of the maple tree sat seven crows. The eighth was perched on the branch closest to the front window, where it had been pecking to get their attention. It turned from the glass and watched with an intent stare, along with its cronies. With eight pairs of black eyes gawking down upon them, it was clear that the crows were dead serious about making contact with Sarah and Addie. Their already bois-terous cawing intensified; the crows obviously had something quite urgent to say.

GET YOUR COPY NOW
http://getbook.at/tailofafeather

WITCH'S TAIL, BOOK 1

Can she awaken her dormant powers and stop a desperate killer destroying the forest? If you like paranormal puzzles, delightful canine companions, and environmental enlightenment, then you'll love Melanie Snow's wagging-ly fun whodunit.

Here's the link to buy the book today!
http://getbook.at/witchstail

HOWL PLAY, BOOK 2

A novice witch. A collie companion. Can this clever duo put noses to the ground to chase down a killer? If you like cute flirty romance, discovering one's true destiny, and love for animals, then you'll adore Melanie Snow's barking-ly fun adventure.

Here's the link to buy the book today!
https://getbook.at/howlplay

TAIL OF A FEATHER, BOOK 3

A mysterious portal. Eight crows with a message. A missing police chief. If you like paranormal puzzles, charming canine companions, and a bit of flirty romance, then you will love Melanie Snow's crafty quest. Take flight into the magical world of Witchland.

Here's the link to buy the book today!
http://getbook.at/tailofafeather

IMPAWSIBLE MISCHIEF, BOOK 4

Stolen charms. A mysterious woman running for mayor. Can beginner's magic save an ill-fated land? If you like wisecracking creatures, enchanting characters, and close-knit sisterhoods, then you'll love Melanie Snow's clever story.

Here's the link to buy the book today!
http://getbook.at/impawsiblemischief

PAWTRAYL, BOOK 5

When a ghost cries murder, an unsolved case could cost her future. Can this witch solve the magical mystery when an old enemy starts casting chaos. If you like wise familiars, heartthrob romances, and mystical whodunits, then you'll love Melanie Snow's paranormal brainteaser.

Here's the link to buy the book today!
http://getbook.at/pawtrayal

Don't Miss Your Free Gift!

Thank you for purchasing *Tail of a Feather, The Spellwood Witches, Book 3*. To show my appreciation and because of a popular request from my readers I am offering a:

Welcome to Witchland Map

https://wendyvandepoll.com/melaniesnowgift

Join Melanie Snow's Paranormal Cozy Mystery Facebook Group

The Wolf Coven

https://www.facebook.com/ groups/melaniesnowcozymysteries

Melanie Snow is the pen name for Wendy Van de Poll, a bestselling author, pet loss grief coach, and animal medium. She is the author of The Spellwood Witches, a paranormal cozy mystery series.

Her books weave together positive magic, snarky forest faeries, and insightful animals with fun and eclectic humor. True life adventures and intuition are woven into her stories laced with unbridled imagination.

She has been followed by wild wolves in minus sixty degrees, hissed at by a mama bobcat, and played ball with a wild owl—among other animal encounters.

Find out more about her work by visiting her at https://wendyvandepoll.com/melanie-snow.

Also get *The Welcome to Witchland Map*.

Download Your Free Gift

https://wendyvandepoll.com/melaniesnowgift

HOW TO FIND MELANIE SNOW

www.wendyvandepoll.com/melanie-snow

www.facebook.com/melaniesnow.cozymysteries

www.instagram.com/melaniesnow.cozymysteries

www.facebook.com/groups/melaniesnowcozymysteries

www.amazon.com/author/melaniesnow

www.goodreads.com/melaniesnowcozymysteries

ACKNOWLEDGMENTS

I would like to thank my intuitive writing team who has guided me to write this fun series. They weren't always easy to deal with but they were patient with my fumbling. Because of them Melanie Snow and all the characters in my head have come to life.

I appreciate all my teachers of the furred, feathered, and finned variety who continue to guide me through life and teach me what matters.

A special thanks goes to my weekly writing buddies H.R. Hobbs and Toni Crowe who are kind, sassy, and amazing authors.

I offer a tremendous amount of appreciation to my beta readers: Nadine, Vicky, and Renee. To my editor

Robyn Margaret Verdugo a huge thank you for your expertise. And thank you to my talented proofreader Allison Rose.

A huge hug goes to my husband, Rick Van de Poll. He is a remarkable poet and human being who dedicates his life to the animals and the environment. He inspires my soul. You can find his books on Amazon, as well.

And of course, Addie. This rescue puppy flew on a jet plane from Texas to grace my life in many ways and writing books with her as a main character is just one. Addie even has her own series called; The Adventures of Ms. Addie Pants on Amazon.